MW01138143

The Hidden House Murders

MISS HART AND MISS HUNTER INVESTIGATE

Celina Grace

This book is for my oldest friend,
Emily Way, with all my love.

Chapter One

I DIDN'T THINK MUCH OF THE house at first sight. It was big enough, I grant you; a large, red-brick stately pile surrounded on three sides by dense forest. As we drove up the winding driveway through the clustered trees, my first thought was that it was too similar to how Asharton Manor had been. Andrew parked the car in front of the front door. This house was nothing like as big as the enormous mountain of stone and glass that made Asharton, mind you. Hidden House was merely a big family home. It would be *our* home, mine and Verity's, for the foreseeable future. I wondered how I was going to like it, living right back in the depths of the countryside again. *Hidden House*. It was an apt name. You would never know it was here, from the main road.

Verity got out first and I scrambled after her, trying to keep my knees together in a ladylike way. I looked up at the outside of the house. A rose bush grew up the side of the front door, although now, in late March, there were no flowers to be seen.

I was growing nervous now, as I always did when arriving at a new place. Verity and I had travelled down from London, firstly by train from Paddington to Winter Hissop, the nearest tiny train station. Andrew, the chauffeur cum footman of our London establishment, had met us at the station, which was a relief. I hadn't been sure how we were going to travel the last five miles and hadn't fancied walking, carrying all my goods and chattels. Not that there were very many of those.

"When does Dorothy arrive?" I asked Verity, somehow finding myself whispering.

She sounded distracted as she answered me. Her face was tipped up and I could only see the curve of her cheekbone beyond the edge of her purple cloche hat. "I'm not sure. Later this afternoon, perhaps, or tomorrow..." She trailed off and began to walk towards the front door.

"Verity!" I said, shocked. "Not the front door."

She gave me an amused glance. "It's fine, Joan. No servants' entrance here. Just the front and back, and I know Mrs Ashford won't mind us using the front." Before I could stop her, she ran lightly up the three brick steps and rang the doorbell.

A woman answered – which surprised me. I was used to butlers. But, I reminded myself, Mrs Ashford kept a small staff. Verity had informed me of that on the train journey down. *All women*, Verity had added with an expressive grimace that made me smile to recall it.

"Ah, Verity," said the lady who'd answered the door. She was obviously the housekeeper. You could tell, not only from the bunch of keys that hung from her belt but from the air of calm authority that she exuded. She was quite a short woman but seemed taller, given the ram-rod straightness of her spine and the set of her shoulders. "And this must be Joan Hart." I stepped forward and bobbed a curtsey. She gave me a quick once-over and nodded once, I hoped, in approval. "I am Mrs Weston, the housekeeper here. Joan, you will report to me directly. Verity, you will do the same, but I know that you know that already. Now, girls, are these all your belongings?" We indicated that they were. "Very well. Andrew, please convey these to the girls' rooms on the second floor."

Andrew began untying boxes and carpet bags from where they were strapped to the back of the car. Dorothy had insisted on her chauffeur accompanying her on this visit, as well as her lady's maid. Apparently, Mrs Ashford didn't drive and didn't own a car. I wondered what the all-female staff would make of Andrew. He was quite young and quite handsome and could probably have his pick. It made me giggle a little inside to think of the flurry his arrival could provoke. I wondered about the women working here. Would they be old, young, middle-aged? Sober or gay? Suddenly, I missed our house back in London and the tightknit group of servants who worked there. Ponderous old Mr Fenwick, the butler, and Mrs Anstells, the housekeeper. The two maids, Nancy and Margaret, and the little tweeny, Doris, who helped me and Mrs Watling, the cook, in the kitchen. I wondered what they were doing in our absence.

I'd managed to gain a place here by the skin of my teeth. I'd been all set to say goodbye to Verity and retain my place at Dorothy's London residence – she wanted to keep her staff on even while she was 'recuperating' in the countryside – but as luck would have had it, the cook at Hidden House had fallen ill and was sent away for her own recovery. She would be away for some weeks, and so Verity and Dorothy had between them persuaded Mrs Ashford to take me on as a temporary cook. I knew Verity had quite a lot of influence with her mistress, but I also prided myself on the fact that Dorothy truly did enjoy my cooking. I was looking forward to running a whole kitchen by myself; no longer a skivvy or even an undercook, but the one actually running the show. I was also slightly nervous. Although I knew my way about the stove and larder by now, this was a new household. I hoped fervently they wouldn't go in for very exotic fare or something faddy, like not eating meat. I'd known a girl who worked in a kitchen for a gentleman who never touched meat. Not even beef steak or something like that. Very odd.

Shaking off my thoughts, I followed Verity and Mrs Weston into the house. From the start, I thought the house had a dull sort of feel to it. I'm sensitive to atmosphere in places. It wasn't a bad feeling, more a sort of...fog about the place. A greyness. There wasn't the feel of this having been a happy family home. It was nicely appointed, if a little bit shabby and worn. Old money – you could tell – but had it been old money that was now running out?

"Follow me, girls," Mrs Weston said, leading the way up the stairs. They were wide, handsome stairs, carpeted in a dull red with brass stair rods and a long sweep of gently curving wood on which to rest your hand as you walked upwards.

Our room was on the top floor, of course; I hadn't expected anything different. At least here, just as at Dorothy's London house, there was only one staircase – not a separate one for servants. That always annoyed me. As we trailed upstairs, behind Mrs Weston's straight back, I caught glimpses of other rooms as we passed them. A wood-panelled room on the ground floor that looked like a study or a library. A large bedroom with a four-poster bed topped with a cream silk counterpane. I wondered if that was going to be Dorothy's room.

"What relation is Mrs Ashford to Dorothy again?" I asked, whispering so that Mrs Weston wouldn't hear me.

"A very, very distant cousin, I think. More of an old family friend." Verity's cheeks were pink from the climb, clashing with her red hair. "She's very elderly, something of an invalid – she doesn't leave the house much. I think she'll be glad of the company."

"Does she know why... why Dorothy wants – needs – to come and stay?" I murmured.

Verity twisted up her mouth. "I'm not sure. As far as I'm aware, she thinks that Dorothy's nerves need a rest and a few months in the country would help."

"Hmm." I wondered whether fudging around the issue would actually help Dorothy. Both Verity and I knew that Dorothy, whilst in need of a rest for her nerves, probably needed more help in battling her over-fondness for alcohol.

But, it wasn't exactly my worry. I meant to help Verity and Dorothy as much as I could, but I was probably better served in making sure that the meals were delicious and timely. The stairs got narrower and steeper as we left the first-floor landing. Here, I would imagine most of the family would have their bedrooms, with the second floor the servants' domain. Still, as places go, it wasn't the worst house I'd been in – not by a long shot.

There was a funny, round window on the second-floor landing, rather like the porthole of a ship. Gentle spring sunshine poured through it, making a dappled circle of light on the wooden floorboards. No carpet up here, just a few rag rugs scattered here and there. Mrs Weston opened the first door off the corridor and gestured for Verity and me to walk in.

It was quite a pleasant room, though not overly furnished and quite austere in decoration. There was an oval braided rug in the middle of the floor, a small dressing table and an equally small wardrobe. The thing I noticed immediately was that there was only one bed. Surely Verity and I wouldn't be expected to share a bed? That little mystery was immediately solved by Mrs Weston's next remark.

"Joan, this is your room and Verity has the one next door." Verity and I exchanged glances behind her back; half gleeful, half apprehensive. It was quite exciting to think about having a whole room of one's own – but might it not be a little lonely too? Verity and I had shared a room for *years*; it would be strange not having her there to talk to late at night or early in the morning.

There was a knock on the door then. Andrew brought my two small cases in and put them on the bed. He flashed me a wink as he left the room, which made me smile as I turned back to start to unpack. The bedstead was the usual iron type, although the counterpane looked quite new and the pillows relatively plump. I remembered one place I'd had where the bedspread had been an old curtain, just the brass rings removed from the top hem. What an old skinflint that master had been, rot him. And the mistress had been just as bad. I remembered the cook had had the eggs counted out for her every morning by the lady of the house. Actually counted out! I could imagine Mrs Watling giving in her notice if Dorothy ever did that to her, not that she ever would. Dorothy may have had her faults but meanness was definitely not one of them.

Verity and Mrs Weston had already left the room – *my* room, how strange it sounded in my head to say that – and I could hear the low murmur of their voices in the room next door. I began to unpack, unfolding and hanging my clothes in the wardrobe where someone had thoughtfully placed some hangers. I put my good pair of shoes on the wardrobe floor. There was only one more thing in my suitcase and I lifted it out carefully.

A bundle of paper, bound in string. I read the words typed on the first page; *Death at the Manor* and then the three words written underneath. *By Joan Hart*. I thought of all the snatched minutes and hours it had taken me to write it, pecking away at the ancient typewriter I had found in a cupboard at Dorothy's London house. Of course, I had checked with her that it would be fine for me to use it. Dorothy being Dorothy had waved a hand airily and told me to throw it out of the window if I wanted to, that old thing. "Type away, Joan," she'd said, "someone in the house may as well make use of it," and she'd lit another cigarette. I held my precious play in my hands and then tucked it back into the suitcase, which I heaved onto the top of the wardrobe.

Pushing thoughts of my play away, I sat down on the edge of the bed to survey my new domain. Wonder of wonders, I had an electric bedside light, with a silk shade, and a small vanity mirror. Even a tiny shelf by the bed for books and ornaments. Feeling content, I got up, unpinned my hat and put it on the shelf. A rose-patterned china jug and washbowl sat on the dressing table but there was no water within it, so I went in search of the bathroom in order to wash my hands. I was glad to see there was a fireplace there – believe me, bathing in an unheated bathroom is not one of life's most comfortable experiences. I suppose, in one way we were fortunate to have a bathroom to ourselves at all, especially in a smaller house.

Verity, myself and Mrs Weston all met in the corridor outside, and Mrs Weston gestured for us to follow her. "I've already arranged for a cold supper for this evening, Joan," she said over her shoulder as she bustled away towards the stairs. "I suggest you make yourself acquainted with the kitchen and introduce yourself to Ethel, who's the maid of all work here. She'll be able to help you get settled."

That was the first, slightly wrong note in my new position. I kept my face neutral and nodded, but I was conscious of a flash of annoyance. I wouldn't even have my own kitchen maid? Verity, who naturally hadn't thought anything of Mrs Weston's remark, given her own position, hummed a little tune under her breath. I tried to be philosophical. This was a small household with an invalid mistress – it wasn't likely that there would be heaps of grand dinners or evening *soirees* to cater for.

The three of us trooped back down the stairs, our heels clattering noisily on the bare floorboards of the first flight of stairs, the sound hushing once we reached the carpeted treads of the main staircase. As we passed through the downstairs hallway, a querulous but aristocratic voice was raised from behind the panels of one of the doors.

"Arabella? Is that you?"

Verity and I glanced at one another. Mrs Weston paused as if hesitating, and then moved towards the door behind which the voice had spoken. "It's I, Mrs Ashford," she said, turning the brass handle. "I'm just showing the new maids to their quarters."

The cracked old voice spoke again, quite imperiously. "Why, then, you must bring them in to meet me."

Verity and I exchanged glances that were somewhat alarmed. It was unusual to be formally introduced to the people you were engaged to work for. One may have encountered them at the interview for the position, but not always, and certainly not in the larger establishments. This would be a first.

Mrs Weston didn't seem fazed by the order. "Come with me, girls," she said, gesturing for us to go forward into what turned out to be the drawing room.

Again, it was comfortably if not luxuriously furnished. The carpet and furniture was a little worn although well maintained. A good fire burned in the grate at the end of the room and beside the blaze, in a green velvet armchair, sat the mistress of the house, Mrs Ashcroft herself.

She was a diminutive figure, more wizened and much older than I had anticipated. It was only as one got closer that one became aware of the undimmed gleam in her grey eyes and the firm set of her jaw, which spoke of someone used to getting her own way.

"And who might you be?" she demanded, as Verity and I got closer. Her left hand rested on the ebony head of a cane, the knuckles of her fingers swollen and bluish against the wrinkled skin of her hand. She wore an old fashioned ruby engagement ring, a cluster of blood-red stones that caught the light of the fire in an answering gleam.

Verity dropped a flawless curtsey. "I'm Verity Hunter, Miss Drew's lady's maid," she said, in the proper, hushed, respectful tone.

"I see. And you, miss?" asked the formidable old lady, turning to me.

I swallowed, less confident than Verity. "I'm –
I'm Joan Hart, the new – the new cook, milady."

"Humph. I'm not a lady. Madam or Mrs Ashford
will do for me." I blinked and nodded. "Mrs Weston
will assist you should you need anything or need
to know of anything. You'll find we run a tight ship
here, but we all pitch in." She favoured us with
another penetrating gaze from those gleaming grey
eyes and then nodded, dismissing us.

Mrs Weston led us out of the room and down the
back staircase at the back of the hallway that led to
the basement kitchen. I was dying to talk to Verity
alone, to find out what she thought about all this,
but it didn't look as though I was going to get the
chance. Mrs Weston ushered me into the kitchen
and, after exhorting me to 'get myself settled in',
whisked Verity away in the direction of Dorothy's
rooms. All we had time for was a wink from Verity
as she went out the door and a grimace from me,
hastily dropped from my face as Mrs Weston looked
back.

The door to the staircase swung back into its
frame as the two of them left. I stood in the middle
of the kitchen floor for a moment, silently assessing
my new domain.

Chapter Two

MY FIRST IMPRESSIONS WERE FAVOURABLE. Although the kitchen was technically below ground, at least on one side, there was a row of windows set high into the back wall that brought the spring sunshine in. The back door was half wood, half glass panes, which brought yet more light to the room. The walls were whitewashed and the floor, thankfully, was of good red ceramic tiles, so much easier to keep clean than the pitted and rough flagstones I'd had to endure earlier on in my life. Quickly, I checked on the equipment. There was a gas stove as well as the range, which was good, but no refrigerator. A door to the side of the kitchen led me to the pantry with its marble-topped shelves. There was a large ice-box and barrels of flour, sugar and tea stood on the floor.

I wondered whether Mrs Ashford herself would meet with me to discuss the daily menus or if she would delegate that to Mrs Weston. It was not a question I would normally have asked, but this was a slightly different household to the ones I'd been used to. I moved around the kitchen, opening drawers, peering into cupboards and trying to acquaint myself with every inch of my new workspace.

I had just located the drawer where the aprons were kept, and was tying one about my waist, when there was a flicker of movement outside the glass of the back door. A moment later, it opened and a woman came into the kitchen.

"Oh," she exclaimed in surprise when she saw me. Quickly, I curtseyed, believing (rightly, as it turned out) that she was Miss Arabella Ashford, the daughter of Mrs Ashford. Verity had told me about her on the journey down. *She's adopted, Miss Arabella. Mrs Ashford and her husband were never blessed with children of their own, but they took on Miss Arabella when she was about seven, I think. She was the daughter of one of Mrs Ashford's friends who was widowed in the war and then died...*

"You must be the new cook," said Arabella, hesitantly. She seemed rather a colourless person: very fair with a washed-out complexion and somewhat prominent pale blue eyes. She was simply – even drably – dressed in a tweed skirt and a limp cream-coloured blouse. She had a sweet smile, though, which I saw a moment later and it brightened her face to something almost pretty.

"Yes, that's right, miss. I'm Joan Hart. I arrived today."

"Um. Jolly good." I got the impression she wanted to walk past me but was unsure of doing so, for some reason. "I must go to my mother—"

"Very good, miss." I bobbed a curtsey again and moved backwards so she could pass me. She gave me another quick and nervous smile as she walked away.

I waited until the door shut and turned back to my tasks. So, that was Arabella Ashford. Thankfully, she didn't seem like the sort of overbearing, interfering type I'd sometimes run up against. There was another member of the household who Verity had also told me about, Mrs Ashford's sister-in-law. Constance Bartleby was a widow and, from what Verity had told me, something of a poor relation. Apparently, she lived with Mrs Ashford as a sort of companion. Idly musing on what she might be like, I decided to go back upstairs to get my book.

Every cook of any note had her own book. It was a collection of recipes, short-cuts, tricks and tips of the catering trade and it was as precious as a Bible. As I climbed the stairs, still a little hesitant about using them, I thought about my play – the collection of papers far more precious to *me*. I still cherished dreams of being a writer, a playwright even, although nobody but Verity knew. I'd never shown her what I'd written. Perhaps I never would.

Perhaps I'd never show anybody. Who was I, anyway, thinking I could write a real play? Even a real book, one day? At that very moment, it seemed the height of silliness. I was just a servant, a cook; that was all.

I found my book, my cookbook and trudged back downstairs, feeling melancholy. I met Mrs Weston coming up the stairs just as I was coming down. Although I knew I had a perfect right to be there, I still felt a little nervous. Mrs Weston was far more forbidding than our usual housekeeper, Mrs Anstells, although perhaps she would warm to me as she got to know me.

"Joan? Are you looking for something?"

"I was just fetching my book," I said hastily, holding it out for inspection. Mrs Weston nodded.

"As I said before, I've arranged for a cold supper tonight. The only family members here tonight are Mrs Ashford and Miss Arabella. But I'm expecting you to prepare the breakfasts tomorrow, and from then on, the kitchen is under your control." She looked at me severely for a moment, as if she wondered whether I'd be up to the task. "You seem quite young to be a fully qualified cook, Joan."

"I'm twenty," I said, unsure whether that would make things better or worse. "But I've plenty of experience."

Mrs Weston's mouth twisted for a moment, as if weighing up the truth of that statement. "Well, Miss

Drew spoke highly of you and we could certainly do with the help whilst Aggie is indisposed."

"I'm sure I'll try and do the best I can." We faced each other in the middle of the staircase.

"No doubt." She looked at me searchingly again for a moment. "Have we met before? Your face looks somewhat familiar..."

I cursed inside my head. She was remembering those newspaper photographs, when the case of the Connault Theatre murders had come to court. Both Verity and I had had to testify and, being young and (in Verity's case) comely, the newspaper interest had been huge. Thankfully, as it had with the Asharton Manor case, the tumult and publicity had quickly died down.

"I don't believe so," I said, with as winning a smile as I could. "Could I just ask you about the tradespeople? Where do I find their contact details?"

"Let me show you." Mrs Weston led me down the stairs and thankfully, her moment of recognition seemed to have passed.

The afternoon passed in a blur of stock-taking, making orders for the morrow, rearranging the kitchen to my satisfaction and introducing myself to Ethel, the maid of all work. She was a plump young thing of sixteen, rather adenoidal, but she seemed a nice enough girl and a willing worker. That was good, because despite it being a small household

17

in terms of the family, there were still five servants, including myself, to cook for.

It was a pleasant kitchen in which to work. The glass-panelled back door looked out onto the gravel drive that ran along the back of the house. At about four o'clock that afternoon, I saw Andrew drive the car past to park it over by the far garden wall. He'd obviously gone to collect Dorothy from the railway station. I wondered, somewhat uncharitably, if she'd got drunk on the train. I'd have to wait until I spoke to Verity later to find out.

It was a tiring day, as new days in new positions are. So many things to remember; rooms and passageways and where the lavatory was located. New names and new faces. Just the smallest things took up one's mind: where the salt cellar was kept, how the tea towels were folded, what kind of china was required for afternoon tea. It wasn't as if I could slope off to bed early either, cold supper or no cold supper. I stayed up late, making sure everything was ready for breakfast the next day. Ethel had the job of getting the range alight and the kettle boiling, and before I said goodnight to her, I reminded her of that. She nodded nervously – she was a bit of a frightened rabbit. Mind you, I remembered my first days in service. I was a-tremble from dawn until dusk, terrified of getting something wrong. I smiled reassuringly at Ethel and dismissed her.

I was climbing the stairs to my room when the

second wrong note occurred. I passed the first floor, where the family bedrooms were located. I could hear the querulous but surprisingly strong voice of Mrs Ashford coming from one of the bedrooms, the second one along the corridor.

"There's no use getting in a pet about it. You can weep and moan all you like, Arabella, but that's an end to it."

Shamefully, I allowed my footsteps to slow. I could hear a female voice answering Mrs Ashford, but it was too low and tear-soaked for me to hear exactly what it was saying.

"There's no need to make a fool of yourself. Why in heaven's name you would think that someone like him would be interested in someone like you, I have no idea—" A soft wail undercut this remark. "Oh, my dear, don't take on so. There are plenty of other young men out there who are much more suited to someone of your – your temperament."

The other voice spoke up and this time I could hear that it was Miss Arabella. "You can't tell me how to live my life—"

"No, I can't, but I'm telling you now, Arabella, you're a fool if you think he cares two buttons about you. And even if he did, he's not the kind of husband that I'd like for you. He may be wealthy but his father's as vulgar as they come."

"You're such a snob." I could hear the anger in Arabella's voice even through the closed door. "You should hear what you're saying. You can't control people like – like puppets, getting them to dance to your every whim, just because—"

I could hear Mrs Ashford's cracked, wheezing laughter. It had a cruel sound to it that made me shiver; less a sound of mirth and more of pleasure in someone else's pain. "Oh, I can, my dear. I've been doing it all my life."

Silence emanated from the room. I held my breath. I knew I should keep walking, that it was none of my business, but I was transfixed by the drama going on unseen behind the wooden panels before me.

After a moment, Mrs Ashford spoke up again and her voice was once more normal, no-nonsense and brisk. The nasty undercurrent I thought I had just heard was gone. "Now, let's not argue with one another. You'll soon see I'm right. I just wish you could understand it before you get yourself hurt."

"You're wrong." I could tell Arabella was starting to cry again.

"Now, come along. You and I both know there's always been one way of changing your mind, so please don't force my hand and make me take that route."

A watery gasp from Arabella. "What – what do you mean?"

"You *know* what I mean, Arabella."

Another silence. Unable to help myself, I pressed my ear to the door.

Then Arabella spoke again, in a dull monotone. "I hate you."

"Oh dear." Mrs Ashford sounded entirely normal, not upset in the slightest. "Yes, that always *was* your response when you realised I was right all along." I could hear her wheezing sigh. It was funny, but listening to her from here, without seeing her, you could almost forget she was old. Her tone changed to something much kindlier, almost wheedling. "Now, now, don't go upsetting yourself. There's no reason why you can't meet someone *much* more suitable. Someone you might even know already. It's not as if you won't have money – that is, if you're willing to—"

A door opened below me in the corridor, and I jumped like a scalded cat, snatching my ear from the door. Heartbeat thumping in my ears, I turned and began to climb the stairs again, trying to run away from the room without making any noise. I really must *not* be caught eavesdropping on my first day in the job. It was a terrible habit of mine, although I knew I was far from being the only servant to do so. One had such little power in life; it seemed only fair to balance it up a bit by being aware of what was going on around you.

I reached my room without incident, telling myself all the way that listening at doors was a little bit naughty but nothing so bad, though I had the uncomfortable feeling I was fibbing to myself.

At least I didn't snoop, I told myself. I didn't read private letters or diaries, or poke around in drawers that didn't belong to me. I'd only started listening because I'd overheard something. I kept trying to justify myself until I realised I had to look away from catching my own eyes in my little mirror. *Think about something else, Joan, and shut up.*

With an effort, I switched my thoughts. So, Miss Arabella was in love with an unsuitable man, was she? Well, she wouldn't be the first, and she wouldn't be the last. I sympathised but not too much. At least she had the time and the energy to actually *meet* someone. Fat chance of me ever having a sweetheart, stuck in front of an oven or a sink all day... For some reason, the face of Inspector Marks came into my mind, and I sighed. Ever since our meeting, during the Connault Theatre murder case, I'd hoped – what had I hoped? That he'd visit me? Court me, even? I blushed to hear myself. There was nothing doing, I told myself firmly. *A man like that wouldn't be interested in someone like you.* I laughed. Those were almost exactly the words I'd heard Mrs Ashford speak to Arabella. Perhaps we weren't so different after all.

I was wearily unbuttoning my dress when there was a knock at my bedroom door and a moment later, Verity's flaming red head poked into the room.

"Joanie. Are you dead on your feet?"

"Very much so." I sat down on the edge of the bed with a sigh echoed by the groan of the bedsprings. "I haven't even done any cooking today and I'm exhausted."

"Me too." Verity came in. Tired she may have been but she still looked wonderfully smart in her silk blouse and wool skirt. Dorothy's cast-offs, yes, but they were of such good quality that they still looked new. I sighed and yanked at the last button. Lady's maids were expected to dress smartly, so I couldn't exactly fault Verity for doing just that, but it always made me feel even more of a dishevelled mess than I already was.

"Joan, you'll have that off. Let me." I felt Verity's gentle fingers free the reluctant button from its button hole.

"Thanks." I peeled the dress off me and hung it up in the wardrobe – now there was a luxury, a wardrobe of my own. I'd been used to a peg rail before.

"Do you think you'll manage? With the kitchen, I mean?"

"I hope so." I thought, with a qualm, of the busy day ahead of me tomorrow. "Is there anything I should know about? Any visitors expected?"

"Ah, funny you mention that. There is." I turned expectantly to Verity, who was primping in front of the dressing table mirror. Her gaze met mine through her reflection. "Mrs Ashford's nephew's expected tomorrow. Him and a Cambridge chum."

"Oh yes?" I felt an extra spurt of anxiety. If the nephew was at Cambridge, then he was almost certainly a young man and, as I knew, young men had prodigious appetites. I hoped we had enough meat ordered from the butcher.

"He's called Michael, Michael Harrison. I can't remember what his friend's name is."

"So, how does he fit in here?"

Verity tucked the last wave of hair in neatly. "He's the son of Mrs Ashford's sister. Not Constance Bartleby, another one. Something like that. Bit of a rogue, apparently, according to Dorothy, but nice with it. She said Arabella's awfully sweet on his friend, whatever his name is." She chewed her lip for a moment, staring into the mirror. "Raymond! That's it. Yes, Arabella's very keen, apparently, but him not so much."

That must have been the man that Mrs Ashford was taking Arabella to task about. "So, Arabella and Michael are cousins?" I asked.

"Well, sort of. Not blood related. Which is probably just as well, as apparently Michael had a bit of a soft spot for Arabella at one point, but she wasn't interested." I listened, trying to sort out all these romantic entanglements out in my head. One thing about Dorothy, she always knew the latest gossip. Verity went on speaking. "No, she didn't want anything to do with him, according to Dorothy. Goodness knows why, as apparently he's really quite handsome."

"Really?" I said, cheering up slightly. Yes, young men in the house may have meant extra work but if they were decorative, then at least you got something out of having to run around after them.

Verity giggled. "Well, you know Dorothy. She's got an eye for a comely young man, hasn't she?"

"How *is* Dorothy?" My curiosity about my mistress was enough to distract me from the worries about the visitors. Although, I supposed that here, Mrs Ashford was technically my employer.

Verity shrugged. "She seems fine, at the moment. She took a sleeping pill and went straight to bed."

I pulled my shawl over my shoulders. "Had she—" I began and then shut my mouth. I wanted to ask if she'd been drinking on the journey down here but really, what business was it of mine? It was impertinent.

Verity looked at me enquiringly. "What, Joan?"

I shook my head. "It doesn't matter. Listen, V, I'm all in. I'm going to get some sleep."

"Rightio." Verity came over and gave me a squeeze. "Do you think you'll like it here, Joanie?"

I yawned. "Sorry. Yes, I think so."

"You don't think the work will be too much? You know, not having a kitchen maid as such—"

I felt a burst of gratitude. She *had* been listening when Mrs Weston had mentioned that fact after all.

"Ethel seems like a likely enough worker. I'm sure we'll manage."

Verity caught my yawn. When she'd stopped, she smiled and said, "Well, it's hardly Asharton Manor, is it, Joanie?"

"Thank goodness." Something occurred to me then. "We're not that far from there, are we, V?"

"Not that far, no." We caught each other's eye, and I could see she was thinking the same thing as I was. "Try not to worry about it, Joan. It's a long time ago now. Another lifetime, almost."

"I suppose so." I thought for a moment of the manor; its golden, treacherous surface, the darkness of the pine forest encircling it. I suppressed a shiver.

"Well, I'm off to bed." Verity flapped a hand at me in a goodbye and sloped off, shutting the door behind her. "Don't let the bed bugs bite."

I continued to get ready for bed. I thought, as I always did, of sitting down and writing something. But, as always, I was too tired. Instead I climbed into the strange bed, clicked off my little bedside light and slid down under the blankets and into sleep.

Chapter Three

THE NEXT MORNING, I WAS *very* glad that I'd prepared so thoroughly the night before. Ethel, like a good girl, had come down before me to get the range going, but as she'd had to dash off to light the fires in all the bedrooms, the stove wasn't nearly as hot as I needed it to be. I thanked my lucky stars that there was a gas stove to cook on as well. At least breakfast was one of the easier meals of the day to prepare.

I helped Ethel carry the dishes up to the dining room. Of course, I would have helped anyway, as there was only the two of us available to wait at the table, but I wanted to have a look at the other members of the household I hadn't already met. And, if I were honest, I truly wanted to see Dorothy, to see if she was well. Privileged, idle and rich she might have been, but our mistress was also kind and steadfast in loyalty to her servants. I didn't exactly admire her, but I liked her.

True to form, as soon as Dorothy spotted me she smiled and said, "Hullo Joan. How are you settling in?"

I smiled back and bobbed a curtsey, having placed the covered silver tray of bacon on the sideboard. "I'm very well, Madam. I hope that everything is satisfactory."

"I'm sure it will be." Dorothy looked over at Mrs Ashford, who sat at the head of the table. She appeared even tinier and more gnarled than she had seemed the night before. Her sparse white hair gleamed under the light from the chandelier.

"Seems somewhat extravagant to me," Mrs Ashford said tartly. "I don't know what's wrong with a good, old-fashioned plate of porridge."

My heart sank. Had I fallen at the first hurdle?

"I'm sorry, Madam," I faltered. "I was following Mrs Weston's orders—" I stopped abruptly, not wanting to sound as though I were making excuses or trying to get the housekeeper into trouble.

"Oh, get along with you, Margaret," said Dorothy, grinning. Mrs Ashford looked affronted at first and then her wizened face collapsed into a mass of wrinkles as she chuckled. Dorothy looked at me. "Don't mind her, Joan, she's nothing but an old curmudgeon."

Astounded at Dorothy's forthrightness, I could do nothing but give a confused bob of the head. Mrs Ashford looked at Dorothy with a kind of wry fondness, and I wondered at the relationship between the two of them. I hadn't realised they were on terms of such familiarity.

Arabella Ashford said nothing during the exchange, merely keeping her eyes on her meal and continuing to fork food into her mouth. Her plate was piled high with eggs, toast, the bony remnants of a kipper, mushrooms and two glistening sausages. It was a wonder she was as slim as she was. She didn't look particularly well this morning, I noted, although she had the kind of complexion that never really looked at its best. I remembered the row I'd overheard between her and her mother. I could still hear that fine needle of cruelty in Mrs Ashford's voice, when she'd laughed about something Arabella had said. I also remembered that dull note in Arabella's voice when she'd responded, belying the violence of her words. *I hate you.*

I hastily recalled myself to the present. The fourth person at the table had to be Constance Bartleby. She wasn't eating but looked from Dorothy to Mrs Ashford, her gaze flicking from one face to the other. She was a stately looking woman, middle-aged but still handsome, with elaborately dressed dark hair and a high colour in her cheeks. She looked faintly foreign. I'd finally got her place in the family worked out, after consulting Verity this morning. She had been the second wife of Mrs Ashford's late brother. As I looked at her, she caught my eye and I dropped my gaze hastily.

"Thank you, girls. You may go." Mrs Ashford dismissed us. As I was at the door, my hand on the doorknob, her imperious voice stopped me. "Oh, Joan. My nephew, Mr Michael Harrison, will be joining us for dinner tonight. He'll be bringing a university companion of his. I'm sure Mrs Weston has the situation under control, but of course I'm relying on you to ensure that we have a suitable meal."

"Yes m'lady—" I stopped myself. "Yes, Mrs Ashford. I took the liberty of ordering a joint of beef this morning, which I hope will be sufficient."

"Oh, good. That sounds eminently suitable. Young men do have such prodigious appetites, don't they? Thank you, my dear." She waved me away with a gnarled hand and I bobbed yet another curtsey and scurried for the door. I sent Verity up a silent prayer of thanks as I made my way down to the kitchen.

After breakfast, there was the washing up to do and a simple luncheon to plan; I settled on soup and a Dover Sole. The servants, here as everywhere, ate far more simply – in this case, breakfast leftovers and extra bread and butter. Throughout the morning, I took delivery of the food for the day, including an icy bucket of fish from the fishmonger and the coveted joint of beef from the butcher. It looked a good cut and I was glad. Roast beef was one of the simplest dishes to prepare for dinner –

the trickiest part was getting the timings of all the side dishes right. I went through the pantry and the larder, looking out potatoes, carrots, swedes and onions. The starter could be something light – a soup, perhaps?

I didn't see Verity all morning but it was not unusual, certainly upon arrival in a new place. She would have been kept busy with unpacking Dorothy's wardrobe; hanging up suits, sorting out gloves and hats and stoles, ensuring the jewellery was safely put away. I found myself wondering exactly what it was that Dorothy would *do* here. She liked parties and the theatre, jazz clubs and all the types of things that couldn't be found in a small country town. But, I supposed, that was the point of her coming away from London; she had to remove herself from the temptations of the high life. Perhaps she would hunt? But then it wasn't the season, was it? Perhaps she would take to drawing, or watercolours, or perhaps even good works in the parish. The last made me giggle at the thought of Dorothy, with her flapper bob and her cigarettes and her racy, expensive clothes, sitting opposite some poor old lady helping her wind her knitting. Or dishing up cabbage soup to the unfortunate in her diamonds and furs. Oh well, it wasn't my concern.

It was about three o'clock that afternoon, and Ethel and I were just sitting down with a well-deserved cup of tea, when there was a rap at the back door. I looked up to see a young man framed in the pane of glass. He was standing in shadow and all I could see was the outline of his cap. Thinking it was another delivery boy, I heaved myself to my feet and yanked open the door.

"Yes?" I said, slightly grumpily.

"I say, are you the new cook?" His accent alerted me immediately to the fact that he was a gentleman. Appalled, I quickly straightened up and removed the frown from my face.

"Yes, sir?" I tried again, hoping he hadn't heard the tone of my voice the first time. My confusion and embarrassment was increased when I realised how handsome he was.

"Hullo there. I'm Michael, Michael Harrison. I suppose the old lady told you to expect me?"

"Yes, sir." I realised that there was another man standing a little way off. Also young, also handsome, but in more of a dark and brooding way, as opposed to Michael Harrison's golden, boyish looks. He must be the university companion, Raymond Something.

Michael Harrison didn't introduce him, which didn't surprise me. Instead, he held out a brown paper bag to me.

"We've been foraging. Thought we'd help out with the old provisions, what? Aunt Margaret just loves mushrooms."

Trying to remain unflustered, I opened the bag.

Inside was a tangled heap of what looked like wild fungi.

I looked up, into Michael Harrison's cheerful face.

"I hope you don't think it's too much of a cheek," he said.

"No, not at all, sir." I *was* flustered, despite myself. Wild mushrooms were all very well, but did this young man actually know what he was picking? One had to be so careful with wild fungi... I couldn't think of a polite way to ask him if he knew what he was doing. I made a split-second decision then that I would carefully check each individual mushroom myself and, if there was any doubt, I'd throw the lot away and use the cultivated ones the greengrocer had already sent over.

Michael Harrison seemed to read my mind. "You needn't worry – I always bring something like this for old Aunt Margaret when I come to visit. You just ask her, that'll take that worried look off your face." He winked at me and I couldn't stop myself smiling. He tipped his hat, turned away and hailed his companion. "Come on, Ray, old chap. Let's get have a wash and a brush-up before tea."

I bobbed an embarrassed curtsey as I watched them walk away. There was a rustle behind me and I turned to see Mrs Weston hurrying into the kitchen.

"Oh, Joan, we'll be needing afternoon tea a little early today. Young Mr Harrison has just arrived with Mr Bentham, and Mrs Ashford wants some refreshments straight away—"

"I know." I closed the back door and hurried towards the kettle. "Mr Harrison was just here. He gave me this." I held out the paper bag for Mrs Weston to take and she must have seen the confusion in my face, because she chuckled.

"That's Mr Harrison for you. He's an outdoor type; loves his hunting and his shooting and grubbing about on the moors and in the forests."

"He said he normally brings some mushrooms for his aunt. Wild ones, I mean."

"Yes, he does if it's the season. A little bit early, I would have said at the moment, but then he knows the best places to look."

Somewhat relieved, I plonked the kettle on top of the range and began to measure tea into the pot. "I'll cook them up for an entrée. I was wondering what to use—" I quickly shut my mouth, not wanting Mrs Weston to hear about any moment of indecision or weakness. "In a cream sauce, I thought."

"That sounds suitable." Mrs Weston sounded as affable as I had ever heard her. She seemed somewhat flurried but, at the same time, in a good humour. "When can I tell Madam to expect tea?"

I glanced up at the clock on the wall. "No more than five and twenty-past the hour, Mrs Weston. I'll bring it up myself."

"Thank you, Joan." Before I could say any more, she hurried out of the kitchen.

Quickly, I made sandwiches – fish paste, jam and gentlemen's relish – chopping off the crusts and setting them to one side for use later. I'd baked scones that morning, thankfully, and there was fresh cream from the milkman and what I assumed was last summer's raspberry jam in the larder. That would do, surely? I fetched the big silver tray from the pantry and loaded it up with all the dishes and cups that would be needed. Before I hefted it up, I checked my appearance in the shiny copper bottom of a frying pan hanging on the rack. My hair was still fairly neat. I pinched my cheeks and nibbled at my lips to try and get a bit of colour in them. Then I whipped off my apron and picked up the heavy tray to take upstairs.

Chapter Four

IT WAS THE SECOND TIME I'd been into the drawing room, which looked a great deal more cheerful this time. Spring sunshine poured in through the windows, dappling the carpet, and a nice little fire flickered in the grate. The whole family, plus their guests, were gathered there, and the room looked quite crowded.

Mrs Ashford reigned supreme, you could see that at a glance. I was reminded of Arabella's accusation of last night, telling her mother she controlled people like puppets on a string. She sat in the same chair by the fire that I'd seen her in before when we'd been introduced. Michael and Mrs Bartleby sat by her and both, in their individual ways, danced attendance on her. In Michael's case, it seemed to consist of telling her amusing stories from Cambridge, and in Mrs Bartleby's, by listening closely to Mrs Ashford's remarks, jumping up to refill her teacup as soon as she saw me enter the room, and by laughing at the slightest hint of humour in Mrs Ashford's comments.

Arabella, Dorothy and Raymond sat on the opposite side of the room, talking nineteen to the dozen. Or rather, Arabella and Dorothy did and Raymond sat and listened. Even though it was only four o'clock, he was already drinking what looked like whisky from a cut-glass tumbler. Both he and Dorothy smoked. Arabella was sitting slightly too close to him to be natural, and it looked as though she would have liked to have sat even closer. I felt a pang of pity for her as I put the tray down on the tea table and began to rearrange the cups and plates. Her eyes were fixed on his face and she laughed too loudly and too long at whatever he said.

I wondered whether I should pour the tea and coffee. Sometimes the family did it themselves. When nobody except Mrs Bartleby approached me, I shrugged mentally and began to pour. At the trickle of tea into the china cups, Dorothy looked over.

"Hullo, Joan," she said, coming up to take a cup. "How are you settling in?"

Bless Dorothy. I tried to sound cheerful and in control as I answered her. "Very well, thank you, Madam. Everything in the kitchen is very well appointed."

"Oh, that's good. Splendid," Dorothy said vaguely. I grinned inwardly. Dorothy wouldn't even know how to boil a kettle, let alone find her way about the kitchen. I watched as she drifted back off to join Raymond and Arabella.

I continued to quietly pour the tea and set out the food and plates whilst keeping an unobtrusive eye on everyone. As always, I was curious about their behaviour and their relationships with one another. Did Arabella have a true affection for her adopted mother? I wondered, remembering Mrs Ashford's tart words to her in her bedroom and Arabella's response. She told her mother she hated her. Did she? From Mrs Ashford's wryly weary response – she hadn't sounded upset – it sounded as if it had been something Arabella had said before. A verbal lashing out, or truly meant?

Mrs Bartleby laughed at something Mrs Ashford had said. I wondered a little about this sister-in-law of Mrs Ashford's. It seemed as she'd lived here with Mrs Ashford for years, her husband having died over a decade ago. I wondered why she hadn't married again. She was handsome enough, but there was something about her I didn't much like, although I couldn't exactly have said what. Perhaps it was her long white hands, and her rather hard face, and the sycophantic way in which she acted around Mrs Ashford. Of course, remembering what Verity had told me, she wasn't wealthy. Quite the opposite. Oh, what business was it of mine? I was probably being very unfair. Not that she would have cared a hoot for my opinion of her, I reminded myself, arranging crab paste sandwiches attractively on a flowery china plate. *Remember your place, Joan.*

My eye fell on Michael Harrison. He was awfully handsome, although I'd never really gone for fair-haired men. I liked them dark and mysterious. Like Inspector Marks, whispered a little voice in my head, and I fought not to blush. Luckily, Dorothy kept coming up and ferrying teacups away with her, so that helped distract me from my bold thoughts. Michael was clearly a great favourite with his aunt, who laughed delightedly at something he said and whose grey eyes were fixed on his face, much as her adopted daughter's gaze was glued to Raymond Bentham's countenance.

I would have liked to have stayed there longer, discreetly eavesdropping on their conversations and watching the interaction between different people, but there was nothing more for me to do, and I needed to be getting on with the dinner. Reluctantly, I dropped a curtsey (which nobody saw anyway – nobody was taking the slightest notice of me) and left the room, closing the drawing room door behind me.

THE REST OF THE AFTERNOON flew by in a whirl of preparation for dinner, both for the family and the servants. I'd been worried about the cream of mushroom soup because that wasn't a dish I was used to making, but it all turned out well in the end. The roast beef was cooked to a turn and I looked at it proudly as I covered it up with the domed silver cover and placed it on the tray for Ethel to carry up to the dining room.

Eventually the servants sat down to eat. It was so much smaller a gathering than I was used to, even smaller than usual as Andrew wasn't eating with us tonight, having had to take the car to the garage in the village to have them change a tyre. Mrs Weston, Ethel, Verity and I sat and ate in a fairly companionable silence. It wasn't that we weren't allowed to talk, it was just I think we were all so tired after our long and busy day it took all our energy just to eat our food. Starting a new position was always exhausting. I looked forward to a few weeks' time, when I would have settled in and wouldn't have to fret myself into a frenzy over the smallest, simplest things.

Verity hung back to help me and Ethel with the washing up, for which I was grateful. Ethel, clearly in awe of Verity, kept casting wide-eyed, sideways glances at her, as if unable to believe that a lady's maid would be getting her well-kept hands dirty. It made me smile despite my fatigue. With Verity's help, we finished in double-quick time, and I sent Ethel up to her bedroom. I could see that she was drooping with tiredness so it was kind of me, but it also meant I could have a cup of tea and a natter with my friend in private.

With the glow of satisfaction in knowing everything was clean, dry and put away, and that things were well in hand for breakfast, I pushed a full tea cup over to Verity and subsided onto a kitchen chair with a sigh. "Thanks for your help tonight, V. It really does make a difference."

"You're welcome." Verity took a sip of tea and her shoulders dropped in a sigh. "Do you think you'll like it here?"

I glanced around, just in case Mrs Weston had hidden herself somewhere in the kitchen. "I'm not sure. It's a little different, isn't it? Not so... Not so..." I found it hard to articulate what I meant. Perhaps it was that here, I didn't feel quite so much like another species – set apart from the wealthy and the aristocratic. But perhaps that was the changing times as much as the new house. Servants were beginning to be treated a little better now, given that there were so many more opportunities for working men and women than just going into service.

Verity seemed to read my mind. "I know what you mean, Joan. The world's changing, isn't it? Even down here in the country, you feel it."

I thought about the new conditions of my position here. No need to wear a cap, although as a cook, I tended to do so just to keep my hair hygienically covered. A whole day off at the weekend and an afternoon off during the week. More money. And it was more than that – it was the attitude of my new employers and the sense that perhaps we were all in this together, in a way. I drank my tea, feeling more cheerful despite my tiredness.

Verity drained her cup, yawned, and pushed it a little away from her. "God, I'm all in. Thank goodness I've already got Dorothy's room ready for when she retires."

"Are she and Miss Arabella close?" I asked, curiously.

Verity shrugged. "I'm not sure. I think Arabella's a bit of a – well, a bit of a stick-in-the-mud for Dorothy." Thinking back on Dorothy's friends in London, I had to agree. "Still," Verity went on, consideringly. "Now that she's supposed to be good, who knows? Perhaps Arabella will be just what she needs." She yawned again. "Mind you, while those young bucks are here, Dorothy might as well be part of the wallpaper. Did you see the way Arabella was looking at that Raymond?"

"He *is* very handsome," I pointed out.

Verity grinned. "Oh, yes, noticed that, did we?"

I kicked her under the table. "I was merely *observing*."

"Of course you were, Joan." She winked at me and got up from the table. "You and Miss Arabella will have to fight over who's going to take him his breakfast tray."

"Verity Hunter!"

"I'm teasing."

I threw a tea towel at her and she ducked, giggling. "Go to bed, you."

Before Verity could answer, there was a creak of floorboards in the corridor outside and then the door opened to reveal Mrs Weston, frowning. Verity snatched the tea towel down from where it had landed on her head. Guiltily, I sat up, wondering if our banter had been overheard and disapproved of.

"Oh, girls, I'm glad to catch you here." Mrs Weston's frown remained but she didn't sound cross – or at least, not with us. "Could you come with me for a moment?"

My stomach sank again. Perhaps we were in trouble after all...

Mrs Weston turned to leave and I sent a grimace over the room to Verity who returned it.

We obediently followed Mrs Weston up the stairs to the first floor, where we stopped outside Mrs Ashford's bedroom. Mrs Weston knocked gently on the closed door, while Verity and I exchanged puzzled glances behind her back.

"Come in," said Mrs Ashford's cracked but imperious voice, and Mrs Weston stood back to let us go into the room. She came in after us and shut the door behind her.

The room was dim, and I saw to my surprise that Mrs Ashford was already in bed, a shawl around her wizened shoulders. Her spectacles gleamed in what little light there was from a small bedside light and the rosy glow of the coals from the fireplace.

"Come here, young ladies."

As we approached the bed, I realised she had a little writing bureau on her lap, one of the wooden ones you could move from desk to desk should you need to. On it, was a document covered with a blank slip of paper. I couldn't see what it was. I had a sudden, paranoid flash that Mrs Ashford had found my play and told myself not to be so ridiculous.

"Now, Joan, Verity, I'd like you to do something for me. All I need is your signature, here and here." She indicated spaces on the paper before her. "Don't be alarmed, you won't get into any sort of bother. It's just I need two people to sign this for me."

And her daughter couldn't do it? Or even Mrs Weston? I glanced back at her, standing statue-still by the door and saw the frown was back on her face and deeper now. She didn't approve of this, whatever it was.

Mrs Ashford must have caught my hesitation. "Don't tell me you girls can't write?" She demanded, incredulously.

"Oh, it's not that—" I bit my lip, holding back what I was going to say. I wasn't best keen to sign something when I didn't even know what it was, but I was hardly going to be able to say no, was I? I could tell Verity was thinking the same thing.

"Well, hurry up and sign it, please." Mrs Ashford sounded impatient. "I'm exceptionally fatigued and I'd like to go to sleep." She repeated herself. "You won't get into any trouble."

Mentally shrugging, I took the fountain pen she held out to me and signed my name where she indicated. Then I handed the pen to Verity, catching her eye. Her face was a wealth of non-expression and for a moment, despite my anxiety and weariness, I had to stop myself laughing.

As soon as Verity had signed, Mrs Ashford snatched the pen back from her hand. "Thank you. You may go."

Mrs Weston held the door open for us and shut us both out after we'd hurried through. I didn't dare look at Verity until we were safely upstairs, out of earshot of the family.

"What the blazes was that all about?" Verity asked, raising her eyebrows and her hands in amazement.

"Who knows?" Suddenly, I was too bone-tired to even talk about it. "Sorry, V, I'm all in. Let's talk about it tomorrow."

She caught my yawn. "You're right. Good night, Joanie."

"Night, V." I watched her shut herself into her room. Then I turned back to mine, all thoughts of that strange little interlude out of my head. All I could think about was getting to bed.

Chapter Five

I WAS FAST ASLEEP THAT NIGHT, too deep even for dreaming, when I was rudely awakened by a hand grabbing my arm and a voice calling me urgently.

"Joan. Joan! Wake up."

I muttered something and rolled over in bed, thick with sleep. The hand wouldn't leave me alone.

"Joan! It's me, Verity. You have to get up. *Joan*."

Verity? Groaning, I forced my eyes open to confront inky blackness. I couldn't see anything in the dark. "What?" I said thickly, trying to wake myself up fully.

There was a noise of impatience and then a bright explosion of light as Verity clicked the bedside light on. I screwed up my eyes against the dazzle, blinking hard.

"V?" I managed to sit up and once my vision had cleared, saw Verity crouched down by the side of the bed, her face tight with worry and a shawl about her nightdress-clad shoulders. "What's wrong?"

"Everyone's ill. You have to come and help me."

"What?" I said again, stupidly. For a moment, I thought I must still be dreaming. As if she read my mind, Verity reached out and pinched the bare skin of my arm.

"Ouch!"

"Sorry, but Joan, I need you to come with me. Everyone is *ill*. I can't manage it all on my own."

"Ill?" I pushed the covers back and put my bare feet to the cold linoleum, my toes shrinking from the contact. "What do you mean?" I spotted my slippers, under the bed, and hauled them out, slipping them thankfully on my cold feet.

Verity flung another shawl around my shoulders – I recognised it as one of hers. "Everyone's vomiting. And worse." She shuddered. "Please, can you help me?"

"Of course, of course." The shock of the cold floor had wakened me fully and we both hastened to the door. "Where's Mrs Weston?"

"She's telephoning the doctor." Verity took my arm and hurried me along the corridor to the stairs. "Dorothy's in a bad way, and I sent Ethel down to Mrs Ashford's room. I haven't even had a chance to check on Miss Arabella—" We were thundering down the stairs by now and Verity almost shoved me in the direction of Mrs Ashford's room. Behind the closed door of the family's bathroom, I could hear groans and retching. I screwed up my face.

"Is it contagious?" I asked Verity. Stupid of

me – she wasn't a physician. I wondered queasily if I was beginning to come down with something myself, although it was probably just the power of suggestion.

"No, I don't think so. I think it's—" Verity coloured and shut her mouth tightly.

"What?" I asked.

She shook her head. "No time for discussion, Joan. I must get back to Dorothy. Can you check on Mrs Ashford and Miss Arabella?"

Before I could say anything, she raced away up the corridor of the first floor towards Dorothy's room. As I stood, flabbergasted, the bathroom door opened and Arabella shakily emerged.

She looked dreadful, white as candlewax with a sheen of perspiration over her face. "Oh, Joan," she said, faintly, and then staggered. Alarmed, I hastened to give her my arm, worried she was going to collapse.

I steered her back to her bedroom and into her bed and, after a moment's thought, discreetly placed the chamber pot near the head of her bed. I left her lying down, her face almost as white as the linen of her pillow, and hurried back towards Mrs Ashford's room. Thankfully, just as I was about to knock and enter, Mrs Weston appeared from downstairs.

"Oh, Joan," she said, looking frantic. "What a to-do. I've telephoned the doctor and he'll be here as soon as he is able."

"But what's happened to everyone?" I asked, feeling rather frantic myself.

"I don't know." Perhaps it was the fraught environment that lent a stiffness to Mrs Weston's tone.

"Can I help—" I began but she waved me aside.

"I shall deal with Madam," was all that she said. "How is Miss Arabella?"

At least I could give her an account of how I'd helped the young woman to her bed. Mrs Weston nodded, her face tight and her mouth folded in like a purse.

"How are the young gentlemen?" she asked, when I paused for breath.

"The young—" I stopped myself just in time. It would be fair to say that I'd forgotten the existence of Michael Harrison and his chum, Raymond Bentham. "I'll go and check on them right away. Um, where are their rooms?"

THE GENTLEMEN WERE HOUSED AT the very end of the corridor on the first floor, Michael Harrison's room next to Dorothy's. As I knocked gently on his door, I could hear the low murmur of Verity's voice in the room next door and it brought me a strange sort of comfort.

There was a silence after I'd knocked and then I heard shuffling footsteps approaching the door.

After a moment, it opened and Michael Harrington's haggard face appeared in the doorway.

"I'm so sorry to bother you, sir," I began. "But I'm afraid everyone appears to be ill and I was just checking that you yourself were—"

He'd been staring at me as if I were speaking a foreign language and just as I began to ask if he were alright, he gave a gasp, a retch and then jack-knifed forward. I jumped out of the way *just* in time.

"Oh gosh, I'm so sorry," gasped Michael from the floor, his head level with my knees. "I'm *so* sorry—"

I overcame my disgust. The poor man couldn't help it.

"Please don't worry, sir. Here, let me help you." Wondering whether I was being too forward and then dismissing the worry – the man was ill and I had to help him – I leant down and helped him to his feet. He clutched at me gratefully.

"Let me help you back to bed..."

"Better take me to the bathroom," he said, with a ghastly attempt at a grin. "Quick as you can."

I gulped and fairly bundled him down the corridor to the bathroom, which was thankfully unoccupied. I virtually heaved Michael into the room and quickly closed the door. He'd have to help himself from now on.

I left the poor man to a semblance of privacy and headed back down the corridor, thinking that I must at least clean up the carpet before I did anything else. My mind was so occupied with thoughts of finding a mop and bucket that the opening of the very farthest door on the corridor made me jump.

Raymond Bentham strolled out, belting his navy-blue dressing gown closed. He looked both sleepy and faintly annoyed but – crucially – he wasn't vomiting and sweating and groaning.

"What the hell's going on?"

I forgave him his bad language. It *was* a bit of a madhouse. "I'm so sorry sir, but everyone's been taken ill. Are you feeling well yourself?"

"I'm absolutely fine. What do you mean, everyone's been taken ill?" He caught sight then of the unpleasant pool on the carpet by my feet. "Ugh. Good God. What is it, food poisoning?"

It sounds silly to say, but that thought hadn't yet occurred to me. I stared at Raymond Bentham whilst the sensation of a heavy weight felt as if it were falling slowly through my body. Oh God... If it were food poisoning, then... "It's my fault," I whispered, almost to myself.

"What's that?" Raymond was looking at me suspiciously. Incongruously, it occurred to me once more how very good looking he was; almost matinee idol good looks.

I swallowed. "I'm sorry sir, but I'm needed downstairs. Are you quite sure you're not – you're not indisposed?"

51

"I tell you, there's nothing wrong with me. Where's Michael?"

"He's, um—" I gestured down the corridor in what I hoped was an eloquent enough gesture. "He's, er, in there."

Raymond got my meaning. He sighed, cast up his eyes and retreated back into his bedroom, shutting the door firmly.

I puffed out my cheeks. Of course, he was a gentleman. I hadn't exactly expected him to pitch in and help, but...it seemed a little *unfeeling* to simply cut oneself off from everybody like that. But perhaps if he were wrong – and I felt a leap of gladness at the thought – about it being food poisoning, and instead it was something contagious that had swept through the house like wildfire, perhaps he was sensible to keep himself apart from those who were already afflicted.

That left Mrs Bartleby to check on. I knocked on the only other door on that floor that could have been hers, the one next to Mrs Ashford's room. There was no answer. I knocked again, somewhat louder, and called, softly at first, "Mrs Bartleby? Mrs Bartleby? Are you well?"

Still no answer. I opened the door and poked my head into the dim interior, dreading what I might see. But the room was empty, and the bed didn't look as though anyone had been taken ill there. The counterpane was pushed back on one side and the pillows were dented but that was all. Where was she?

She must have gone to the bathroom already. But no, Michael was in there; she couldn't be there. Where on earth was the woman? She must have slipped off to another bathroom, perhaps even the servants' one upstairs. I thought for a moment of going to look for her and then dismissed the idea. If she were well enough to leave her bed, she was well enough to look after herself for a moment. I really needed to get that carpet clean.

I turned back, determined to find some cleaning utensils, and almost ran straight into Verity, who had just emerged from Dorothy's room. Her arms were piled high with a load of soiled sheets.

"Is everything all right?"

Verity rolled her eyes. She looked exhausted but thankfully didn't seem to be ill. "Dorothy's not so bad now. I think she's got rid of everything that she could. There's nothing left to come up."

I grimaced. "I need to find a mop and bucket. Do you know where they're kept?"

"I think so. I need to get these in to soak, anyway." We both began to hurry towards the stairs. I could hear Mrs Weston talking inside Mrs Ashford's room but without being able to hear what she was saying. I felt a qualm – should I go in and try and help? But Mrs Weston was an efficient woman, and she'd been with her mistress a long time. No doubt she had the situation under control. The doorbell rang just as we reached the hallway and although I wouldn't normally have taken it upon myself to answer it, I made a guess that it would be the doctor. As it happened, I was right, and I directed him upstairs to Mrs Ashford's bedroom before hastening after Verity, who had disappeared down the kitchen stairs.

Chapter Six

IT WAS ALMOST LIGHT BY the time Verity, Mrs Weston, Ethel, myself and Doctor Goodfried sat down to a much-needed cup of tea at the kitchen table. None of the servants had been taken ill, thankfully, but we all looked just as dreadful as if we had; haggard, sweating, dark semi-circles under our tired eyes. Nobody spoke until we'd all drained our cups and I wearily got up to refill the teapot with some more hot water.

Mrs Weston sighed. "My goodness me, what a dreadful night."

Doctor Goodfried replaced his teacup on the saucer with a clink. "I think the worst is over now. I'll engage a nurse to come in for a few days. Mrs Ashford will need some specialist care."

Mrs Weston looked worried. "Is she very bad, Doctor? She seemed more…more at peace, when I left her."

"She's had a bad run of it, and of course, being so elderly, she's bound to suffer more. Miss Ashford and Miss Drew seem to be slightly better. Mrs Bartleby seems to be sleeping quite peacefully, and I'll double-check on Mr Harrison before I leave." He inclined his cup hopefully towards me, and I quickly poured him some more tea. "Thank you, my dear." He seemed a nice man, rather round and tweedy, like a bearded teddy bear. "Now, I suppose we really need to get to the bottom of what happened."

I grew cold. Should I say something? But what could I say? Would it be better to bring up the subject of food poisoning myself, so that it looked as though I didn't have anything to hide? I *didn't* have anything to hide. If I had, in fact, poisoned half the household, it had been entirely inadvertently. *Courage, Joan.* I took a deep breath.

"Sir, I..." Despite myself, my voice failed. I cleared my throat and tried again. "Doctor, I – Mr Raymond said something about food poisoning. Do you think – is that what you think happened? Because if it is, then I must – I must have caused it..." To my shame, I found myself close to tears and had to stop talking. Verity sat next to me and a moment later I felt her hand in mine beneath the table, giving it a quick, friendly squeeze.

Mrs Weston looked forbidding but the doctor wasn't quite so intimidating. "I really don't know, Joan, my dear. It could very well be food poisoning. What was it that you gave them for dinner? I note that all the servants seem to be unaffected. Presumably they had a different menu to yours?"

Ethel's teacup rattled on its saucer. We all looked at her in surprise and she blushed and said "Sorry. My hand slipped."

I recollected myself. "Yes, that's right. The Ashfords and their guests had, um, roast beef for the main course. Roast potatoes, peas, carrots, onions to accompany that. A lemon tart for dessert." I was thinking hard, trying to remember what I'd cooked. "Oh, and I did a mushroom soup for the starter. Mr Harrison brought me some wild mushrooms that he's collected on his journey down and Mrs Ashford asked me to use them."

Doctor Goodfried's bristly eyebrows shot up. "Wild mushrooms, eh? Hmm." He rasped his fingers along the edge of his beard. "Well, they may well have been the culprit. Did you get a close look at them?"

I nodded. I had checked them thoroughly before I cooked them and had seen only harmless, edible varieties. One of the few memories I have of my father was of him taking me on walks in the countryside and the two of us picking mushrooms. He'd taught me the right ones to pick and the poisonous ones to leave well alone. I told the doctor as much. I could feel Verity's surprise next to me. I'd never told anyone about that before. It was such a precious memory because I had so few of my father.

I had none whatsoever of my mother as she died when I was born.

"Could you have been mistaken, Joan?"

"I suppose so," I said, feeling that honesty was always the best policy. "I looked carefully but I suppose there's always a margin for error."

"Hmm. And you had no suspicions about the beef?"

If I had, I would scarcely have cooked it, let alone served it, was what I didn't say. Instead I shook my head. "None whatsoever. It was a very good quality joint and I'm confident I cooked it well."

I sounded more confident than I felt. Not about the beef – of that, I was sure that it had been just fine, not least because I'd eaten some of it myself (I *do* like roast beef). That thought made me pause for a moment. Had anyone eaten the mushroom soup that hadn't become ill?

I said as much to Doctor Goodfried. He raised his eyebrows again and nodded.

"It will be the work of a moment to ascertain that, my dear. Leave that with me."

"Mr Bentham wasn't ill," I said, rather hesitatingly. Although what I was saying was the truth, it did sound a bit – accusatory. But what was I accusing him of?

"Indeed." Doctor Goodfried drained his second cup of tea and put the cup back down again. "Ah, that hits the spot. Right. I suppose you don't have any of the soup left?"

"I think I do." I was so tired I couldn't quite remember then if I had saved some. "I think I saved some – I was going to use it as the basis for a stew later..."

Mrs Weston looked approving at this frugality. Trying to shake the tiredness off, I got up and looked for the pot that had contained the soup. It was hard to find. Eventually, I spotted it in the sink, filled with cloudy water. "Oh," I said. "I'm sorry. I must have used it all up and put the pot in to soak."

"Oh well, it can't be helped," said Doctor Goodfried. "I'm not sure what good it would do anyway."

I looked to Mrs Weston for guidance. "Do you want me to prepare any breakfasts, Mrs Weston?"

Doctor Goodfried interrupted before she could answer. "I'm afraid that would not be a good idea. No, the patients must eat nothing today but take plenty of water, tea perhaps – plenty of fluids."

Mrs Weston nodded, exhaustedly. She had that transparent look that true fatigue gives the skin. I knew just how she felt. "Joan, please ensure that there's bread, butter and cheese for the servants. We'll have to make do with that this morning." She looked at me with the first sign of compassion she'd ever shown. "I think you girls should go to bed and try and get a little rest. We'll all be needed later."

I knew that perhaps I should protest and offer my services but I was just too tired. I was virtually swaying on my feet, and I could see that Ethel and Verity were similarly afflicted. Too tired to feel anything but a dull relief, I nodded, fetched the foodstuffs from the larder and left them on the table.

"Well, I'll be off," said the doctor, getting up. "Mrs Weston, please tell your mistress, if she's awake, that I'll call back later this afternoon. Please do telephone me if anything changes." He paused for a moment, looking sombre. "Especially if anyone gets worse. Keep a particular eye on Mrs Ashford. She's had a bad go of it and she's elderly and frail."

Mrs Weston nodded, looking worried. The doctor tipped his hat to us all and left, escorted by the housekeeper.

Us three girls looked at one another.

"Blimey," said Verity. "What a night."

Ethel said nothing. It struck me that she was looking particularly uncomfortable.

"Ethel?" I said, quite sharply. "Are you well?"

She blushed and nodded. "I'm fine, Mrs Hart."

I was going to press her further but a swamping wave of exhaustion stopped me. I was just too tired.

"Let's go up then," I said and began the slow climb up to my room, my tired feet barely able to carry me up the stairs.

Chapter Seven

WE WEREN'T ALLOWED TO SLEEP the day away. By two o'clock that afternoon, Mrs Weston came knocking at my door, rousing me from a deep slumber.

"Joan. *Joan*. Time to wake. Joan. Wake up."

Groggily I sat up. I had pulled the curtains against the spring light and the room was dim. Even so, I could see Mrs Weston's pallor through the gloom. I blinked myself awake. "I'm awake, Mrs Weston."

"Good. Could you please return to the kitchen and make up something suitable for the invalids?" She turned, stumbling slightly. "I'm going to my room for the next hour."

I supposed she hadn't yet had any sleep herself. I felt something I'd never felt for her before: pity. "Of course," I said as cheerfully as my sleepy voice would allow. "Please don't worry, Mrs Weston. Between Verity and I, we can keep things ship-shape." She was too senior for me to be able to urge her to go and rest but I willed her to do so in the privacy of my own head.

When she'd gone, I dragged myself out of bed, groaning. I'd taken off my dress but kept my petticoat and chemise on. I splashed water on my face from the bowl on the dressing table and blotted the drops off on the towel I kept folded next to it. The morning fire in my room had long since died and I shivered in the chill, hastily buttoning my dress and trying to fight my hair into some semblance of neatness.

Verity poked her head around the door just as I was pushing the last hairpin into my hair. "Oh, you're up," she said blearily.

"So are you." I looked at her more closely. "Or at least, I think you are."

Verity yawned. "I'm dead on my feet. We've just got to get through the rest of the day and then we can go back to bed, thank God."

"How is Dorothy?"

Verity shook herself and sighed. "She's better. Quite a lot better. She's sitting in with Arabella and Mrs Bartleby at the moment."

"What about the young gentlemen?"

Verity grinned. "Why, want to minister to the sick?"

I threw a hairpin at her. "I'm merely *asking*."

Verity sobered up. "I think Mr Michael is asleep. That Raymond is down in the study playing billiards."

I rolled my eyes and then remembered something. "He *didn't* get sick, did he?"

"No. Dorothy asked him whether he'd had any of the soup."

"And had he?"

Verity grinned again. "Apparently, his exact words were "Mushrooms? Never touch the damn things. They're disgusting.""

"Well, it was probably lucky for him that he felt that way." I looked at my reflection in the little mirror. My eyes looked worried. *Had* it been the mushroom soup? It must have been, I told myself. Everything else was fine.

"*You* didn't have any of the soup, did you, Joanie?"

I shook my head. "No. I tasted it, of course. But there wasn't enough for the servants as well."

"Lucky for us." Verity shivered theatrically.

"Yes." I regarded myself for a second longer, obscurely troubled. Then, shaking off my anxiety, I joined Verity at the door and we made our way downstairs.

ETHEL, GOOD GIRL, WAS ALREADY in the kitchen, stoking up the range. The kettle was throwing clouds of steam into the air. I fell upon it like a parched traveller throwing themselves into a desert oasis. What on earth did working people do before tea was discovered and brought to England? I asked Verity as much.

She yawned and shut her mouth with a snap. "Sorry. They drank beer, I think. Small beer."

"Now, that I could appreciate." The three of us giggled and then shut up abruptly as Arabella Ashford came into the kitchen. She looked wan but better than she had last night.

"Oh, Joan, I was wondering if you had a tray I could take up to Mother. She's feeling a little better and doctor thinks she should try and have something light to eat."

"I'll make one up straight away, Miss." I tried to cudgel my fuzzy brain into working. "I've yet to make up a broth but I could cut some bread and butter and beef tea won't take long to make at all."

"Thank you." As she spoke, her pallor increased alarmingly and she swayed, putting a hand out to steady herself on the kitchen table.

Verity took charge. She was experienced in coaxing Dorothy to do whatever it was she had to do, and someone like Arabella was even easier to persuade. "Miss Ashford, I think you should be back in bed. You look terribly pale and we wouldn't want you collapsing here, would we? Let me help you back to your room."

"I need to take Mother her tray..." Arabella whispered.

"Joan can do that," Verity said firmly She looked

at me for confirmation and I nodded and echoed the words.

I could see Arabella felt too ill to protest. I watched Verity lead her gently but firmly away to the stairs and turned back to the stove. I could use the remnants of that roast beef for the beef tea. I would test it first by eating it. Paranoid, I knew, but the last thing I wanted was for everyone to get even sicker.

I set Ethel to making up the servants' meals and something for Raymond Bentham, whose appetite was in no way diminished. Mrs Bartleby seemed quite recovered too, although had apparently gone back to bed, according to Verity on her return to the kitchen. It was then I remembered her mysterious absence in the chaos of the last night. Where had she been? Not that it mattered. I reminded myself that she'd probably gone upstairs to use the servants' bathroom as I made up a tray of scrambled eggs, toast and tea for her. Then I made a start on the vegetable broth. The two nurses Doctor Goodfried had promised us had already arrived, and they would no doubt need endless trays of their own, if they were anything like the other nurses I had worked with in previous places.

ONCE EVERYTHING WAS UNDER CONTROL, I fetched one of the big silver trays from the pantry and set out everything that Mrs Ashford might need upon it. A delicate china cup and saucer, a small silver teapot, a wisp of steam rising from its spout. A plate of bread, spread corner to corner with best butter, the crusts cut off. A rolled napkin encased in one of the bone napkin rings from the kitchen dresser. I would normally have put a bud vase with a single flower in it on the tray but unless I went outside grubbing for daffodils, there weren't a great deal of flowers available this early in the year. I decided Mrs Ashford was probably feeling a bit too poorly to worry much about flowers on her tray anyway.

"I'm just going to take this up to Madam," I said to Ethel, who was scrubbing away at the porridge pots, her round cheeks scarlet with the effort.

The tray was heavy and I climbed the cellar stairs carefully. I could hear the music coming from the study; some rather raucous jazz on the gramophone. Raymond Bentham amusing himself, no doubt. I carried on up to the first floor, setting the tray down on the hallway floor before knocking gently at Mrs Ashford's bedroom door.

There was no answer. I bit my lip and tried again, knocking a little louder. I could hear the sound of female voices coming from Dorothy's room. Still no response from Mrs Ashford. To hell with it. I opened the door, picked up the tray and gently nudged it open with my foot.

"It's just me, Madam, with your tray."

Again, there was no answer. I sensed a stillness emanating from the room; something intangible that raised the hairs on the back of my neck. *She's just asleep, don't panic*. I swallowed and edged further into the dim room. I stood still for a moment, letting my eyes adjust to the darkness, trying to remember what it had looked like when Verity and I had been in here the night before. Could it really have only been the night before? Our signatures on that piece of paper... For the first time, I realised what that paper could have been. A will? Or something else completely? I could see that the heavy velvet drapes were drawn tightly against the sunlight but a single shaft of golden light had slipped through and dust motes whirled and danced in the beam.

The big, four-poster bed was directly ahead of me. The covers were rumpled and thrown back but the bed itself was empty. Puzzled, I stood still for a moment. Then, realising Mrs Ashford was probably just in the bathroom, I moved forward again, balancing the heavy tray. There was a chest of drawers over near the window, and I walked towards it, thinking that I must at least put the blasted tray down before I dropped it.

I walked past the end of the bed, glanced over at the dying embers of the fire, and promptly gasped. It was almost a scream, except the breath was driven from my lungs in what felt like a hard blow.

67

Mrs Ashford lay on the rug in front of the fire, face down and motionless.

How I didn't drop the tray then, I don't know. Shaking, I lowered it to the carpet and then hastened over to Mrs Ashford. She was terribly still; so still, in fact, that I think I knew then, before I even touched her, that she was dead. I reached trembling fingers out to her fragile neck. She was still warm and, for a moment, I was filled with a rush of relief. I spoke her name. "Mrs Ashford? Mrs Ashford? Can you hear me? Are you all right?"

A stupid question, I know, but I wasn't thinking straight. Now I was close to her, I could see the blood in her hair and on the edge of the hearthstone. I couldn't see if she were breathing. I put a hand on her back, the bones of her ribcage frail as a bird's beneath my fingers. No pulse, no heartbeat. Even as I felt for her pulse again, I could feel the warmth ebbing away from underneath my fingertips. Frantically, I looked around for help, as if there were any to be had. Over by the bed was a pair of slippers, one kicked sideways. Had Mrs Ashford stumbled over them as she got out of bed? Stumbled and fallen and hit her head? It seemed likely. She was old and frail and had been very unwell. Perhaps she'd had a fit or something and had hit her head on the hearthstone as she fell. Oh, Lord. What a calamity. I felt absurdly guilty, as if by coming into the bedroom, I had caused this all to happen. If I'd just stayed outside, would Mrs Ashford even now be slumbering peacefully in her bed?

Don't be absurd, Joan. I spoke to myself as sharply as any Mrs Weston could. Mrs Weston! That was who I had to tell and straight away. I jumped to my feet. The small, frail body of Mrs Ashford lay before me and I hated to leave her, so vulnerable and exposed in her white lawn nightgown, but I knew I mustn't move her or touch her any more than I already had. I took one last, desperate look at the former mistress of the house and then ran for the door.

Chapter Eight

As I ran past Dorothy's bedroom door I felt an urge to go in and get Verity to come with me. I felt I could use the support. But I knew that I mustn't. Lady's maid she may have been, but the housekeeper reigned supreme, and I knew Mrs Weston would never forgive me if I undermined her authority.

I stopped for a moment, confused. Why was I running this way, down to the bedrooms of the young gentlemen? Mrs Weston's room was on the top floor, along with my own room, Verity's and Ethel's. I could hear faint snores coming from behind Michael's bedroom door and of course Raymond was downstairs in the study. Shaking my head and starting to realise that I was beginning to tremble from the shock of discovering the body, I wheeled about and ran for the stairs.

As luck would have it, I met Mrs Weston on her way down the second-floor stairs. She was fully dressed in her usual black, the dark circles under her eyes still pronounced. But she did look a little bit more rested.

"Joan," she said, frowning. "What on earth is the matter?"

Now that I came to tell her, I found myself quailing. How long had Mrs Weston worked for the family? I had the impression it had been a long time. Had she cared for her mistress? No doubt she would be shocked and horrified, no matter how strongly she felt or not.

I gulped some air into my lungs. "Mrs Weston, I'm so sorry. Could you – could you please come with me?"

MRS WESTON DIDN'T CRY OUT when she saw poor Mrs Ashford, but she gasped. I stepped a little closer to her, to catch her if she fainted. But she was made of sterner stuff than that. She approached the body with trepidation and stretched out a hand. She didn't make contact. The hand stayed in the air, hovering above the poor, shrunken body, and began to tremble. I looked at her face and could see the glassiness of tears in her eyes.

After a long moment, she spoke hoarsely. "We must fetch the doctor."

I braced myself. She wasn't going to like what I said next. "And the police."

Mrs Weston whipped her head around to look at

me, startled. "Oh, I don't think we need to do *that*. Why on earth would you—" She turned her head back around to look once more on Mrs Ashford. "No, we must fetch the doctor."

I didn't feel the need to press the point. I thought Doctor Goodfried had seemed knowledgeable and efficient enough. He would drive things forward if necessary.

"Should I inform Miss Arabella?" I murmured.

Mrs Weston looked even more shocked, if possible, than she had before. "No, indeed. What an idea, Joan. I will do that."

I preserved a discreet silence. Mrs Weston wasn't to know that it wasn't the first time I'd encountered a dead body. "I'll go and make some tea," was all that I said.

I wasn't sure if Mrs Weston even heard me. I left her staring down at the body, tears running down her face and turning spots on her black dress even darker.

THE KITCHEN FELT LIKE A place of refuge. I filled the kettle and slammed it down on the range. As I waited for it to boil, I attempted to gain control of my emotions. Was I fated always to end up working in a place where somebody died? I scoffed at myself but the unease remained. But surely there was nothing suspicious about this death? Mrs Ashford was an old, sick, feeble lady. It's not your business, I told myself, staring fiercely at the boiling kettle as if it had offended me personally. *Leave it to the doctor to decide what to do.*

Just as the whistle of the boiling kettle built to a scream, Verity walked into the kitchen.

"Tea! Thank God, Joanie."

She looked pale but not unduly upset. For a moment, I felt dizzy. Was this still really the same day? So much had happened and we'd all only had a few hours of sleep. No wonder I was feeling so anxious.

"You've heard the news? About Mrs Ashford?" Verity nodded but didn't answer. There was so much I wanted to know. "How is Dorothy?" I braced myself for the answer, expecting to hear about hysterics and tantrums and general weeping and wailing. Not that I could exactly blame Dorothy – she'd lost her mother and her brother to murder and a sudden death would be bound to bring all the bad times back – but I always felt it was jolly hard on Verity, who was the one who had to stand firm under the onslaught.

Verity sighed. "Sad. Subdued. She's still not very well but she's taken it hard. Mrs Ashford and she were close." She went and fetched one of the trays and began to help me in laying out cups and saucers. "She'll be better for a good pot of tea."

"She's not – drinking?" I asked, timidly. It felt

73

like a cheek to even enquire but Verity didn't get cross.

"No, she's not. Of course, it helps that there's barely anything in the house."

I nodded in understanding. "And – and Miss Arabella?" Given the complexity of the relationship I'd sensed between her and Mrs Ashford, I wondered what her reaction would be.

Verity sighed again. "She's devastated. Well, understandably." She put the last teacup on the last saucer. "I'm not sure how Mrs Bartleby is. Mrs Weston was just going to break it to her as I came down here."

We grew quiet then as we continued to set out the tea trays. Luckily, I'd filled the kettle to capacity. I poured boiling water into each of the pots, lifted them onto the trays and shrouded them each with a cosy. The cosies themselves were knitted in bright wool, in alternating stripes, and I wondered for a moment whether they were slightly too frivolous for the occasion. Then I told myself not to be so silly. As if anyone would be worrying about the colour of a tea-cosy at such a moment.

Verity took up Dorothy's tray and I lifted the one for Miss Arabella (and Mrs Weston, who I thought had looked as though she were in dire need of a cup). As it happened, Arabella was sitting in Dorothy's room, white and shaken. Dorothy sat next to her on the bed, rubbing her back. At first, I thought Dorothy was ill, she was so wan and pale. Of course, she had *been* ill but Verity had said she was better...It was only after a moment that I realised it was possibly the first time ever I had seen Dorothy without a full face of make-up.

Her eyes met mine as I brought in the other tray. All she said was "Oh, Joan," but that was all she needed to say. She may have been my mistress, aristocracy to my lowly origins, but right then and there, we understood one another. We'd been through it all before: Dorothy, Verity and I. We three had been through so much together. That meant something, and I felt a rush of affection, and yes, respect, for her that brought tears to my eyes.

"I'd like to take Mrs Weston a cup, madam," I murmured. "Where is she? In Mrs Bartleby's room?"

"Yes, of course you must. Poor Mrs Weston." Dorothy drew the sobbing Arabella into her arms and spoke to me over her shaking shoulder. "No, I think Constance and she are – I think they're – she's..." She fell silent and indicated with a tilt of her head that Mrs Weston was in Mrs Ashford's room. I nodded and curtseyed in silent understanding.

I knocked gently at the door to the late Mrs Ashford's room. After a moment, Mrs Weston's hoarse voice said, "Come in."

I held the tea cup in my hand and tried to hold it steady. It was difficult, entering a room in which I knew there was a dead body. Mrs Weston looked ravaged – there was no other word for it. Pity for her rose up in my throat and almost choked me.

"I thought you might need a cup of tea, Mrs Weston," I said, holding it out like a peace offering. Mrs Weston was still standing in the same position by Mrs Ashford's body as she had been when I left the room earlier. Mrs Bartleby sat in an armchair by the wall, so still and silent that for a moment I hadn't realised she was there. "And a cup for you, Madam," I said hastily. "I'll just fetch it from the other room."

Mrs Bartleby didn't answer me. In fact, I'm not sure she even heard me. She was staring at the body of Mrs Ashford with a blank look on her white face.

"Thank you, Joan," said Mrs Weston, faintly. I almost had to put the cup into her hands and close her fingers around it. "Thank you," she said again, and tears were not too far from her voice. It was the touch of kindness that did it, I could tell. You can be strong as long as someone isn't kind to you, and then you just crumble.

I managed to edge Mrs Weston over to one of the dressing table chairs and gently but firmly ensured she sat down. She subsided rather quickly and I guessed that she was feeling quite weak. I hesitated, unsure of whether I was forgetting my place in the suggestion I was about to make. "Should I – should I telephone the doctor, Mrs Weston?"

I braced myself for anger but there was none.

She shook her head, weakly. "I've done so already. He'll be here as quickly as possible." She raised the trembling teacup to her lips and took a minuscule sip. "I had to come back here. I didn't want to leave her."

I didn't quite know what to say to that. Wondering again if I were being over-familiar, I patted her shoulder. She didn't seem to take offence.

"Joan, I'll have my tea in my room," Mrs Bartleby said abruptly. Her voice was as hoarse as if she had a cold. Both Mrs Weston and I looked at her as if we'd forgotten she was in the room. We watched as she stood up unsteadily and made her way to the door, fumbling for the door handle as if she were blind. "I'll be in my room."

As the door shut behind her, a voice I recognised as Arabella's suddenly raised in a wail in the room next door. I winced and Mrs Weston jerked in her seat. I could hear the murmur of both Verity and Dorothy's voices as they, I assumed, attempted to soothe her.

"I must go to Miss Arabella. I shouldn't have left her after I told her but... Miss Dorothy was there and she said to leave her and – and I – I didn't realise Mrs Bartleby was in here. I felt I just couldn't leave Madam on her own." Mrs Weston looked ill. She tried to rise, and I quickly assisted her in doing so. "Joan, please stay here until I return. I can't bear the thought of – of Madam being on her own."

"I'll stay," I said hastily. "The doctor will be here very soon, I'm sure."

"Yes. I'm sure you're right." Mrs Weston seemed to pull herself together a little, although she was still a little unsteady on her feet as she made for the door.

After she'd gone, I heaved a sigh. Then I tiptoed to the window and drew back the curtains, desperate for some daylight. Being in here in the semi-darkness with a corpse was something to try the strongest of nerves. Then I turned back.

Something on the carpet caught my eye. I frowned and moved a little closer. It was very faint, so faint that I almost was convinced my eyes were tricking me. But were they? I went closer and knelt down, careful not to disturb what I was looking at. The pile of the rug seemed to be slightly ruffled. Barely noticeable but now I had more light to see, it *was* noticeable. Was it a drag mark? I leant even closer, squinting hard. It *looked* like a drag mark.

I sat back on my heels, feeling suddenly colder. Had the body been moved? Or was I imagining things?

The door to the bedroom opened and Mrs Weston came back in, this time accompanied by Doctor Goodfried. I hadn't heard the doorbell but I'd been concentrating so hard on the carpet that I must have not heard it ring.

"Thank you, Joan," said Mrs Weston. "You may return to the kitchen now."

Doctor Goodfried gave me a nod as he passed me. I opened my mouth to say something about the mark on the carpet and then shut it again. It wasn't my place. I took one last look at the sad little tableau on the carpet and headed for the door.

Chapter Nine

FOR ONCE, THE NEXT MORNING, I was glad of the hard work awaiting me in the kitchen. It allowed me to free my mind from worrying and fretting about what had happened, and it helped me to get myself back under control. The usual kitchen tasks of food preparation – washing and chopping and frying and baking – were soothing in their repetitiveness. I also took some comfort in making sure I provided a suitably sombre but easy to eat lunch for the family. Nothing too chewy, nothing too meaty. A light soup, fish pie and greens and a delicate lemon tart for pudding. I wasn't expecting Miss Arabella to eat much, if anything, and the same probably went for Dorothy, but I was less sure about the young men. Perhaps Mr Michael was still feeling under the weather but Mr Raymond seemed unperturbed by either illness or Mrs Ashford's death.

Mrs Ashford's body had been collected and driven away in a black mortuary van. I supposed that there would be a post mortem, perhaps, although as it was not being considered a suspicious death, perhaps I was wrong. I thought once more of what I thought I'd seen on the carpet. Had my tired eyes been playing tricks on me? Had I *really* seen it? Perhaps it had been a trick of the light or a fault in the weave of the carpet. I pushed the thought away from me more than once that day; I was too busy and too tired to think through the implications.

That evening, I was washing my face at my dressing table when there was a light knock at the door. Before I could answer, the door opened and Verity came in. I had barely had a chance to talk to her all day, and I was so glad to see her, I flung my arms around her in a fierce hug, wetting her shoulder with my damp face.

"Joanie, ugh!"

"Sorry." I swiped at my cheeks with a towel. "How are you? How is Dorothy?"

"I wanted her to go to bed but she's still taking care of Arabella. *She's* prostrated, poor girl."

"She must be glad that Dorothy is here."

Verity rolled her eyes. "Well, her cousin's not exactly been of great help, has he? Mind you, he's still not well."

I thought of the dinner plates that had come back down to the kitchen, the food on them mostly untouched. "I suppose not."

"And that Raymond's about as much help as a wet weekend."

"He's a man. *And* a student." I thought of Mrs Bartleby, who'd spent most of the day in her room. Was it grief, or idleness, or recovery from her illness? How ill had she been, anyway? I remembered looking for her that night everyone became sick. Well, it wasn't important. I began to unpin my hair and brush it out. "Has the doctor said anything to Dorothy?"

"About what?"

Now it was my turn to roll my eyes. "About poor Mrs Ashford of course."

Verity looked startled. "Why? What have you heard?"

"Nothing. That's why I'm asking you. I've been slaving over a hot stove most of the evening."

Verity flumped down on the edge of my bed and the springs groaned beneath her. "I saw the – the body being removed. As far as I'm aware, Doctor Goodfried thinks she had a fall."

I nodded. That did seem the most likely explanation. Again, I pushed aside that momentary unease I'd felt when I'd seen that mark on the carpet. I was just too tired to start looking for shadows that weren't there.

"Well," said Verity, yawning. "I think I'll turn in now that Dorothy's unlikely to need me. It seems like we've been up for about a week."

I caught the yawn. Was it really only the night before last that everyone had become ill? So much seemed to have happened since then. "I'll do the same. I can scarcely keep my eyes open."

"Good night then."

"Good night, V."

I flapped a tired hand at her as she went out of the doorway. Then I kicked off my slippers, turned out the bedside light and fell thankfully forward into bed.

STRANGELY, I WAS AWAKE THE next morning long before I ought to have been. Perhaps it was the increasingly light mornings and the sweet spring songs of the local birds that woke me. Perhaps it was something else. I lay there for a moment, in my narrow bed, and drew the counterpane up to my chin. It was chilly in my room without a fire and I knew it would be a while before Ethel came to light it.

Go back to sleep, Joan, while you can, I urged myself, but it was no good. I was as wide awake, as if I'd swallowed a pot of very strong coffee. Sighing, I got up and bundled myself into my dressing gown; it was a good thick woollen one that Dorothy had given me once for Christmas. It made me giggle a little to think of her buying it – it was so obviously something she wouldn't be seen dead wearing, being made of a tweedy blue plaid. It was so unlike the satin and silk wraps that she favoured, but I was very grateful for it all the same. These old houses really held onto the cold. I pushed my feet into my slippers, watching my breath plume into the chilly air.

The house was silent as I made my way downstairs. I had noticed that before, after a death; a kind of stillness. A hush falls over the house, muffling sounds, dampening down the atmosphere. I cast a glance at Mrs Ashford's room as I passed it. The image of the drag mark on the carpet reoccurred to me. I *had* seen it, I realised that now. It had been a drag mark. Frowning, I made my way all the way to the kitchen and began to stoke up the stove. Technically it was Ethel's job, but it wouldn't hurt matters to make a start.

The kettle eventually boiled and I poured myself the first, marvellous cup. I remembered Mrs Watson, Dorothy's London cook, saying to me once, "I don't ever really taste that first cup of tea – it goes down too fast." I knew just what she meant. Fortified by that first cup, I began to think about the day ahead, but try as I might, I couldn't push the image of that drag mark on the carpet out of my head.

All right. Think, Joan. What does it mean?

I sat at the kitchen table, sipping my second cup as I thought. Had the body been moved? *Why* would it have been moved? That didn't make sense. Mrs Ashford had died from a fall, hitting her head on the corner of the hearthstone, so why would her body have been moved?

I was just beginning to reach a glimmer of understanding, a cold twinkle of perspicacity, when Ethel came hurrying through the kitchen door, completely distracting me from my thoughts.

"Ooh, sorry, sorry Mrs Hart. Sorry, I overslept—"

It still gave me a jolt to be called 'Mrs Hart'. Of course, I knew that cooks, along with housekeepers, were awarded an honorific, despite their marital status or lack of it, but it still seemed strange to me. I made up my mind.

"You don't have to call me that, Ethel. I'm quite happy for you to call me Joan."

Ethel blushed and muttered something I couldn't quite hear. Again, I was reminded of her jumpiness at the table yesterday. But perhaps that was understandable, given the circumstances.

I assumed, in the lack of any other instruction from Mrs Weston, that the breakfasts would go ahead as normal. Ethel and I began to prepare them.

Verity came down into the kitchen at five and twenty-past eight. She looked tired but less shattered than she had last night. She gave me a weary smile as she waited for me to pour boiling water into the silver teapot on Dorothy's tray.

I set the teapot down, suddenly determined to speak out. "V, have you got a minute?"

"Not really." Verity, despite that, looked enquiringly at me.

I jerked my head towards the walk-in pantry. "One minute. That's all I ask."

We scurried into the tiny space, crammed in on all sides by tins and packets, and I shut the door. Verity raised her coppery eyebrows. "What's wrong, Joan?"

I sighed. "Well...it's nothing – it's probably nothing – *but*..." I told her, as quickly and as precisely as I could, about the drag mark I'd seen on the carpet of Mrs Ashford's room.

Verity frowned. "But what would that actually mean?"

I'd been thinking about that myself. "Well, could someone have moved the body? Moved it to the position in which it was found?"

Verity's frown grew deeper. "Why? Why would someone do that?"

I'd been thinking about that too. I took a deep breath. "Because perhaps Mrs Ashford didn't hit her head on the hearthstone at all?"

A silence fell. I could clearly hear Ethel clattering the pots and pans in the room next door. Verity held my gaze for a long moment.

I couldn't stay silent. "Don't look at me like that."

Verity huffed and looked away. "Like what?"

"Like – like *that*."

Verity looked annoyed. "Well, why not say what you really mean, Joanie?"

Our gazes met and melded. "Which is?"

"You don't think Mrs Ashford died a natural death."

There. It was out there. I took a deep breath. "I'm not saying that."

"Well, what are you saying?"

"All I'm saying is that it looked as though somebody has tried to move the body."

There was another silence. Then Verity breathed out sharply through her nose, her nostrils flaring.

"What?" I snapped.

She shot me a look that was perilously close to dislike. "As if we haven't got enough to worry about." Shaking her head, she turned on her heel and groped for the door handle. "Just – just—"

"What?"

Verity's mouth pinched. "Why do you always have to go looking for trouble, Joan?"

I was flabbergasted. "I – I don't—"

"So, *don't* then." The final two words were almost spat at me. Verity wrenched at the door handle and was gone in a flip of red hair and outrage, leaving me behind in the pantry, speechless and upset amongst the bottles and cans.

Chapter Ten

WELL, THAT PUT A BIT of a dampener on things, as you can imagine. I didn't see Verity for the rest of the morning, which was probably just as well. Luckily, Ethel and I were kept busy. Everyone's appetites seemed to have returned, and the two nurses being in the house also made for extra work. They like their trays, do nurses.

It didn't help that Ethel seemed somewhat distracted. She kept dropping things; things that didn't matter, like whisks and saucepans, and things that rather did, like eggs. After the second one plummeted to the tiles to shatter in an oozing pool of white and yolk, I'd had enough.

"Ethel, what *is* the matter?"

She blushed even harder. "Nothing Mrs – Miss – Joan."

I hesitated, wondering whether to take her up on it. But then I heard footsteps on the stairs and the moment passed. "Well, clean it up then," I snapped, reaching for the kettle and feeling an urgent need for a cup of tea.

The footsteps turned out to belong to Doctor Goodfried and Mrs Weston. She ushered him into the kitchen. I noticed he cast an appreciative glance at the steaming kettle.

"Could you make the doctor a cup of tea, please, Joan?" Mrs Weston asked. She glanced around the kitchen but, thankfully, all was under control.

"Of course." I set out the cups and a plate of biscuits that Ethel had baked that morning. Doctor Goodfried tucked in without ceremony. Mrs Weston stood there for a moment. I was about to ask her a question about the dinner that evening but something in her face stopped me. She looked... lost. As if she'd suddenly forgotten where she was or perhaps even who she was.

It was only a moment's reflection. She seemed to come back to herself and bustled away. I watched her go uneasily.

Doctor Goodfried drained his cup with a sigh and prepared to get up. "No rest for the wicked," he said. "I'll be popping back in later, to check on everybody, but I think I can safely say that the worst is over."

He didn't mention Mrs Ashford, but why would he to me? I hesitated, wondering whether to say something about my suspicions. Then, remembering

Verity's tart words to me that very morning, I shut my mouth again.

The doctor picked up his black leather bag from the floor and was heading for the stairs when, to my utter astonishment, Verity and Dorothy came into the kitchen. I think the doctor was as taken aback as I was.

"Miss Drew? Are you all right?" he asked.

Dorothy waved a languid hand. "I'm really quite well again. It was just—" She sought me out with her gaze. I risked a look at Verity, who looked serious but not unduly annoyed.

Doctor Goodfried waited expectantly. Dorothy smiled and flapped a hand at me. "I think Joan has something to tell you."

I gaped. Me? What did Dorothy mean?

Dorothy seemed to understand my hesitation. "Go on, Joan. Tell the doctor what you told Verity."

"I – I—" I stuttered like a fool. Then I saw Verity give me the ghost of a wink and that made me pull myself together.

I glanced at Ethel. "Ethel, can you go and check for more eggs, please? I don't believe the gardener's brought them in this morning. Here, take this basket."

Once she'd been sent on her way and out of earshot, I took a deep breath. Then I told the doctor what I'd told Verity, no more, no less. I'd seen a drag mark on the carpet by Mrs Ashford's body and it was my opinion (I almost faltered over this bit but managed not to) that somebody may have moved the body.

Doctor Goodfried did me the courtesy of listening to me without interruption. When I'd finished speaking, he asked the obvious question. "Why would somebody do that?"

"I don't know," I answered honestly. "But I've been wondering whether to mention it..." I caught Dorothy's eye and she gave me a slight, very slight nod. "It's not my place to speculate, sir. But I do think I should have mentioned it."

Doctor Goodfried regarded me for a moment. "Well, perhaps you're right, Joan. Very well. You can leave that knowledge with me."

"Very good, sir. Doctor." I felt a proper idiot now. What on earth did I think I was doing, thinking that it was up to me to start casting doubt on what was very probably a completely natural death? What had Verity said? *Don't go looking for trouble, Joan.*

But she'd obviously told Dorothy. And Dorothy had considered it worthy of comment. Dorothy had considered me trustworthy. But then, we'd all been through this kind of thing before, hadn't we?

With a small start, I realised the doctor had gone and Dorothy with him. Verity still leant against the dresser, her arms folded across her chest.

I looked her in the eye. "Thanks, V."

Her mobile mouth twisted in something that

could have been humour. "Well, on reflection, you're often right about this sort of thing." She rolled her eyes. "Sorry about this morning."

"You – I could understand why you feel like that. And I don't know about being right but – well – thank you."

Her smile grew. "God knows what's got into Dorothy, though. I would have thought she'd have run a mile from any suggestion of – of wrongdoing."

I sat back down at the table and poured myself the dregs of the teapot. "She seems...different, here."

Verity pushed herself away from the dresser. "I know. It's odd..." She trailed off and I waited for her to elaborate but she didn't. After a moment, she tucked in a red curl and said, in a brisker voice, "Anyway, I've got to go."

"Thanks, V. Really."

She rolled her eyes at me again and left, leaving me smiling and a little relieved that our minor spat seemed to be over.

I began to clear up the kitchen table, thinking about Verity. We quite often had cross words. Verity had a temper, and although I prided myself on being more on an even keel, I was well aware that I could get snappy and irritable myself, particularly when I'd been working harder than usual. I realised I missed sharing a room with her. The novelty of having a space to myself had worn off and I often went to bed feeling a bit lonely.

The back door opened and Ethel puffed in with a basket full of eggs.

"Good girl," I commented, aware that I'd been more than a bit short-tempered with my kitchen maid than perhaps she'd deserved. She was only a slip of a thing, really (albeit a fairly *hefty* slip of a thing). Scarcely more than a child. She shot me a shy smile and went to put the eggs away, and we passed the rest of the day in our respective tasks in a more amiable and comfortable mood.

Chapter Eleven

I FULLY EXPECTED VERITY TO COME to my room that night after putting Dorothy to bed. I even made a pot of cocoa, in one of the less valuable tea-pots and carried it up the stairs to my bedroom, along with two mugs. But she didn't come, and after drinking the whole pot of cocoa by myself, and trying to distract myself from sleepiness with a book, eventually I heard the creak of her bedroom door next to mine as it was opened and shut. She didn't pop her head in, or knock on the wall, or anything. I sighed and turned out my bedside light, both a little anxious and annoyed. Was she angry at me for making more of this death than perhaps I should? Or had she just had a hard day with Dorothy and needed quietness and solitude? It could so easily be the latter. Dorothy may have encouraged me to tell what I knew to the doctor but that didn't mean she was unaffected by what had happened. I thought back to all the death that had visited her establishment, in one guise or another, and shivered.

Of course, the blasted cocoa meant I was up and down to the lavatory half the night and spent the next morning yawning hugely over the stove. Ethel still looked jumpy as a rabbit. I made up my mind, between yawns, that I was going to have it out with her the moment I got a second to catch my breath.

After lunch, Ethel and I were tackling the washing up between us when Verity popped her head into the scullery.

"Have you got a moment, Joan?"

I wiped my wet hands on a tea-towel and headed for the door. "Of course."

Out in the kitchen, Verity jerked her head towards the corridor. "Is there anywhere more private we can go?"

"Um—" I looked around. "Not really. What is it?"

Verity widened her eyes. She was dressed very smartly this morning, in a dark blue dress that brought out the creamy tints of her skin and set off the colour of her hair. I, inevitably, looked down at my stained apron and felt the bedraggled ends of hair on my neck and sighed. "The local bobby's coming over this afternoon, apparently. He wants to talk to Dorothy – and you."

"Me?" I pulled my lips back from my teeth in a grimace. "Oh, help. Does Mrs Weston know?"

Verity shrugged. "I'm not sure. But I just wanted to warn you."

I nodded. I was about to ask her something else when she gave me a wink and hurried off, a shaft of sunlight catching her hair as she ran through it in a flash of copper.

I mentally shrugged and made my way back to the kitchen. Ethel had almost finished the washing up. I helped her put the last of the crockery and cutlery away and then filled the kettle. "Sit down for a minute," I suggested. "Let's have a cuppa and take the weight off our feet for a moment."

Ethel smiled gratefully. I decided that this was as good a chance as any to ask her what was bothering her. I didn't go so far as to actually make her tea – that *was* a skivvy's job – but I gave her a big smile and said, as warmly as I could, "Thanks for all your help here, Ethel. It's made my life a lot easier."

This was stretching the truth a bit but a bit of flattery never hurt anyone. Ethel almost blushed and sipped her tea through a smile.

I took the bull by the horns. "Is there anything bothering you?"

Immediately, her shy smile fell away. "No – No, Miss – Mrs – Joan."

"Come on," I prompted. "You've been nervy as anything the last few days. What is it?" I hazarded a guess. "I know it's been awful here with poor Mrs Ashford's passing away and all the sickness—" I stopped, because her colour had deepened. "What, Ethel?"

She was almost the colour of one of the red poppies on Dorothy's silk dressing gown. "Um... Um..."

"Come on, girl. Out with it."

Ethel gulped. "Well, Mrs – Joan – that's just it. It's the – well, when everyone was sick from the mushrooms, it... I—"

I was beginning to feel impatient with her incoherence. I took a deep breath. "What about it?"

Ethel looked frightened. "Well, Mrs – Joan – you know you were looking for the rest of the soup – the mushroom soup – to give to Doctor, well – I—"

She stuttered to silence again. I nodded encouragingly.

Ethel gathered her courage. "Well, it was me, Mrs – Joan. I ate the rest of it. I'm ever so sorry."

She looked as though she were about to burst into tears. With difficulty, I kept a straight face. "You ate it?"

Ethel gulped again. "Yes. I'm ever so sorry. I don't know what came over me, I was that hungry."

I forced my mouth to look stern, which was difficult, as I felt like shrieking with laughter. All that worry and angst about a little bit of soup! "Well, there's no harm done, Ethel. Next time, ask me though, please? I was going to use it for one of the dishes the next day." A thought occurred to me.

"Still, it was probably just as well I didn't, given how everyone reacted."

Ethel nodded fervently, clearly relieved to have escaped a dressing down. "Yes, miss. Sorry, Joan."

I drained the dregs of my tea. "That's fine. Well, we'd better get on."

I don't know why it took so long for the penny to drop. I must have been tired. It wasn't until I was well into setting the bread for the next day that it occurred to me. I gasped and stood still for a moment, hands frozen on the breadboard in a cloud of flour.

Ethel was chopping vegetables beside me. She looked up at my exclamation. "What is it?"

I took a grip of myself. The ramifications had clearly not occurred to Ethel, and I wasn't about to enlighten her. I had to be sure myself. "Um... *You* weren't ill, yourself, were you, Ethel? The other night?"

Ethel shrugged her shoulders a little. "No, I was fine."

"Well, that's a relief." I almost laughed as I realised I meant the exact opposite. But I didn't want to alarm Ethel and so began talking of the dinner menu and what we had to do before supper. I was still talking nineteen to the dozen when there was a knock at the kitchen door and we both looked up to see a uniformed constable in the doorway.

I'D BEEN EXPECTING HIM, THANKS to Verity's

warning, but it was still a shock. I recovered myself quickly though and greeted him. He introduced himself as Constable Palmer.

"I understand you have something to tell me, Mrs Hart?" He was quite a pleasant looking man, perhaps thirty-odd, with a thick thatch of sandy brown hair. The oddest thing was that he looked faintly familiar too. Surely we couldn't have already met? He didn't have the local accent, that was true, but where on earth would I have met him before?

All these things went through my mind like lightning as I wiped my hands on a tea-towel and gestured to the constable to sit down at the kitchen table. Ethel hung back, looking frightened again. I gave her what I hoped was a reassuring smile. "Ethel, you can have five minutes to please yourself. Why not go and get some fresh air?"

After she'd scurried off, I turned back to Constable Palmer. He still looked familiar. It was on the tip of my tongue to ask him if I knew him when he forestalled me by asking his own question. "So, you have some concerns about Mrs Ashford's death, do you, Mrs Hart?"

I didn't abuse him of the honorific. I thought it might give my testimony more weight. He didn't sound as though he was humouring me; he sounded honestly interested. *Thank you, Dorothy.*

I poured him a cup of tea and sat down myself and told him all I knew, which didn't sound like much. He listened and nodded gravely and made copious notes in his little notebook.

After I'd said all I could on the subject of the body being moved, I hesitated. Should I tell him about the soup? But why not, I asked myself. Surely that was one piece of evidence that pointed to the death being suspicious? The annoying thing was that I hadn't had a chance myself to work out exactly what it might mean...

"There's one more thing," I said slowly. Constable Palmer, who had been in the process of putting away his notebook, looked up. "I've only just realised – I mean, I've only just found this out myself. So perhaps it's nothing." I cursed myself inwardly. Why did I always second guess myself? I knew jolly well it wasn't nothing.

"Please do say, Mrs Hart."

"Well, Doctor Goodfried thought that the reason everyone became ill was because the soup had contained poisonous mushrooms." I hesitated. I could sense the drama inherent in my next few words. "But I don't think that can be the case, because my kitchen maid – you just saw her, Ethel – she ate the rest of the soup. And she wasn't ill."

Constable Palmer regarded me. "Just talk me through that one more time, Mrs Hart. From the beginning."

I did so, simply, without embellishment. Constable Palmer asked very few questions but the ones he did, I was able to answer. After I stopped speaking, we regarded each other for a moment, in silence.

I was the one to break it. "So you see, perhaps that changes everything."

Constable Palmer nodded slowly. Then he became brisk, putting his notebook neatly away in his breast pocket and pushing himself to his feet. "You can leave that with me, Mrs Hart."

Now I had a qualm that perhaps I'd gone too far. "Of course. I know it's not my place..."

He smiled, inclined his head and began to leave. I stopped him with my voice. I just had to know. "I'm sorry, Constable, but have we met before? You seem awfully familiar."

He smiled again. "We have indeed, Mrs Hart. I used to work at Scotland Yard, under a friend of yours, Inspector Marks."

I froze again, my teacup halfway to my lips. Inspector Marks. It had been months since I had seen him but I'd thought of him every day. "Scotland Yard?"

Constable Palmer nodded. "Found the pace a bit much for me up there, to be honest. Then the wife inherited a cottage in the village here so we moved down." He looked at me keenly. "I remember you well, Mrs Hart. The Inspector always said—" He stopped suddenly, leaving me agog at what he had been going to say.

"Well, golly," I said, rather feebly. "What a small world."

Constable Palmer regarded me for a moment longer. Then he nodded again, quite briskly, and said, "You can leave everything with me now, Mrs Hart. Thank you for your help. I'll see myself out." And leaving me to chew over the minor bombshell he'd just thrown my way, he tipped his helmet to me once more and was gone.

Chapter Twelve

I HAD TO SPEAK TO VERITY that evening, Dorothy or no Dorothy. As luck would have it, Dorothy and Arabella went out that evening – to the pictures, I believe – and so I was able to grab Verity and haul her off to my room once I could be sure that Mrs Weston wasn't going to object to the maids finishing work for the evening.

"What is it, Joan?" Verity looked amused as I hustled her into my room and shut the door behind her.

"I need to talk to you." I wished I'd made another pot of cocoa, this time for us to share, but I hadn't the energy to trek back down to the kitchen again. I wondered what would it be like to have a servant of my own. Someone at my beck and call, someone to do my bidding. *Chance would be a fine thing*. I dismissed those silly thoughts and turned to my friend, who sat down on the edge of the bed and began to undo her shoes.

Verity yawned. "Gosh, my feet. It's no joke being

in heels all day." I didn't bother to ask her why she didn't wear flatter shoes. Dorothy wanted a *chic*, well-turned out lady's maid, and that meant smart shoes for Verity, all day, every day.

"Listen." I sat down next to her, the springs creaking musically under me. Then I lost my nerve. What if she got cross with me again? Was my new theory something she would actually want to hear?

Verity rubbed one stockinged foot. "That Michael and his good-looking young chum are off tomorrow, I hear. Back to university. Although they'll have to come back for the funeral."

I hadn't thought about Mrs Ashford's funeral. I wondered, given the new knowledge that I'd passed onto Constable Palmer, whether it would take place as soon as first expected. "Oh, yes?" I said, vaguely.

"Although Lord knows when that will actually *be*," said Verity, almost reading my mind. "They haven't even read the will yet."

The will. Something else I hadn't considered. Suddenly, I was convinced that the piece of paper we'd signed on the night of the poisoning *had* been a will. I opened my mouth to say something and then shut it again.

"Come on, what's eating you?" Verity asked. "Spit it out."

That reminded me of Ethel and what she had told me earlier. I took a deep breath. "Listen, V –

Ethel told me something today which I think could be important."

Verity's smile dimmed a little. "Which is?"

I took another deep breath. "Well, you know how everybody got sick—"

Verity rolled her eyes. "Don't remind me."

"Sorry. But, you know they did. Remember Doctor Goodfried said that it was mushroom poisoning?"

Verity frowned. "Well, I didn't know that he actually said that—"

I waved a hand. "Perhaps not in so many words, but that was the assumption."

"I suppose so. I suppose it was a reasonable one."

I nodded. "Well, they couldn't test the soup because there wasn't anything left of it. I thought I'd kept a bit back – I was going to use it in a stew the next day – but I couldn't find it and I thought I'd been mistaken."

Verity was listening alertly now. I was suddenly catapulted back in time, to when we'd discussed our other...cases, I suppose you could call them. All those memories of how we'd worked it out, both of us contributing in our own way. I was suddenly flushed with pride and the ache of nostalgia.

"Go on, Joanie," Verity promoted, and I realised I'd stopped speaking.

"Well, anyway, Ethel confessed to me today that she'd actually eaten the rest of the soup. She was

hungry and so she'd eaten it and then she was too
frightened of me to confess."

Verity's mouth twisted in humour. "You're so
terrifying, Joan."

"That's not the point," I said, annoyed that she
didn't see it. "Ethel didn't *get sick*. At all. She was
absolutely fine."

Verity's face remained puzzled for a moment,
and then it cleared, very slowly, as the knowledge of
what I was saying began seeping into her features.
"Oh," was all that she said.

"So, whatever made everyone sick can't have
been the mushrooms," I said, just in case that hadn't
occurred to her.

She gave me an annoyed glance. "Yes, I realise
that, Joan." She was quiet for a moment and then
asked, "So, what do you think it was?" She answered
her own question. "It must have been something
else they ate."

"It wasn't," I said. I'd been through this with
Doctor Goodfried. "We – the servants – had the rest
of the food too. We were fine."

"So, what *was* it?"

Our eyes met. I became aware that I was biting
my lip.

"I don't know," I answered, honestly. It was true;
I *didn't* know.

Verity put a hand to her temple. "Have you told
the police this?"

I nodded. She let her hand drop back to her lap, as if the strength had gone out of her arm. "Well, that's all you can do."

I bit my lip again, this time in frustration. I wanted to thrash out the possibilities, talk through what might have happened and why, but I sensed that she didn't want to. Perhaps she was wise. It was late, and we were both tired and really, what was there to actually *know*? Several of the household had got ill. Mrs Ashford, a frail, elderly lady had had a fall and died. That was it.

"Well," I said, slightly artificially. "I just wanted to let you know. But it probably doesn't mean anything."

Verity didn't say anything, but she put her arm around my shoulders and gave me a squeeze. Then she got up and picked her shoes up from the floor. "I'm off to bed, Joanie. Have a good sleep."

"Good night." I smiled at her as she left. Still sitting on the edge of the bed, my eyes fell on my suitcase on top of the wardrobe. Then they dropped to the notebook I kept by the bed. Yes, I would do some more writing tonight, I decided. It was my first attempt at a book, this time, and I'd told nobody about it, not even Verity. If anything could take my mind off possible crime, that could. Fired with enthusiasm, I undressed, got into my nightgown, and got into bed, nestling my notebook on my lap and reaching for my pen.

IT WAS A BEAUTIFUL MORNING, the next day; golden, clear and sunny. I set to preparing the breakfasts with Ethel's help and renewed enthusiasm. I'd written almost a whole chapter last night and I was pleased on two counts – one, in that I'd managed to write something, several pages, in fact, and two, I was happy with what I'd written, in the main. I fried bacon, wiped mushrooms and beat eggs whilst picturing my future. Should I send off the play I'd already written? Should I just at least try to do *something* with it? I flipped the sizzling slices of bacon, picturing my name in lights at a theatre in the West End (well, why not? If one is going to imagine something, one may as well make it worthwhile). Imagining great actresses and actors of the future falling over themselves to land a part in one of my plays, newspapers giving me glowing reviews... It was silly, but it was fun and the morning's work had never flown past so quickly. Ethel seemed far less jumpy now she'd revealed her guilty secret, which helped. Clearly, the ramifications of what she'd confessed hadn't occurred to her, and I wanted to try and keep it that way.

I carried the breakfast dishes up to the dining room myself, wanting to make sure everything was just right. It had been a topsy-turvy time since poor Mrs Ashford's death, with some people eating breakfast in bed, some wandering into the dining room just as I was hoping to start clearing it (Michael and Raymond were particularly guilty of this). But today, as I returned to the dining room with the last serving of toast in the white china rack, I could see that everyone was gathered around the breakfast table. Arabella still looked like a ghost of herself, and she wasn't eating much either. Dorothy at least looked fully recovered from her illness, and the young men seemed back to their chipper selves. Mrs Bartleby looked wan but in control of herself. As I prepared to leave the room, I was struck by the fact that nobody particularly appeared to be grieving, except perhaps Arabella. Mrs Ashford had been respected, perhaps, but not particularly loved. Sad but not particularly unusual. I took one last look at the breakfast sideboard, checking everything was in place, and turned to go.

Mrs Weston came into the room and there was something in her stance, a coiled tension in her straight shoulders that communicated itself, firstly to me and then, I could see, to the rest of the room. Arabella started, her hand closing in a fist on her napkin.

Mrs Weston looked ill. "Miss Ashford, may I request an audience with you?" She seemed oblivious to the other guests staring at her. "In private?" she added.

Arabella unclenched her fist. "Of course," she muttered, getting up and moving swiftly towards the door. Mrs Weston followed her, shutting the dining room door behind her.

I flung a glance at Dorothy. She frowned and appeared deep in thought. Then she looked up and saw me. "Oh, Joan. I think I've had enough to eat. Could you tell Verity to come up to my room? I need to get dressed."

I nodded. Michael buttered toast with what looked like cheerful unconcern but I saw his eyes dart to the closed door. Raymond did, at least, appear oblivious to the tension in the room. Mrs Bartleby's hand quickly replaced her teacup onto her saucer, the musical chink of crockery meeting crockery ringing out across the room.

I walked quickly towards the kitchen where I knew Verity was having breakfast. As I passed the study, I heard the murmur of voices behind the closed door. As I passed it, there was a sharp cry of "No!" which I knew must have been Arabella. Mrs Weston's voice came quickly, raised but attempting to soothe.

"I'm sure it's just procedure, Miss. I don't really see how we can say no..."

Burning with curiosity, I knew that I couldn't stay and eavesdrop. I hurried downstairs to where Verity, bless her, was just rinsing off her dirty plate in the scullery. She turned and caught sight of my face. "Golly, Joanie, what's wrong?"

"I don't know. Something's happened." I told

her what I'd overheard, adding that Dorothy was looking for her. Verity looked annoyed.

"Blast, I can't call my soul my own. Honestly, Dorothy's five and twenty years old. You'd think she'd be capable of flinging a dress and some earrings on by herself, wouldn't you?"

I stared at her. I'd never heard Verity speak like that about her mistress before. She caught my eye and flushed. "Oh, ignore me, Joan, I'm just a bit fed up at the moment."

"What's wrong?"

Verity stared down at the plate in her hand. "Oh, nothing. Everything. You know."

I didn't, really, but I could sympathise. She handed me the clean but wet plate, rolling her eyes, and said, "See you later, Joan. We'll talk then." She was gone before I could even say another word.

I began to clear the kitchen table and tried to think about what I had to do that day in terms of food. It was difficult. What was it that I had heard Mrs Weston say? *I'm sure it's just procedure...* Did that mean something to do with Mrs Ashford's death and Constable Palmer's visit yesterday? Or was it something completely unrelated? Something to do with the funeral arrangements?

I came to with a start, realising I was stood like a statue by the kitchen table with a damp cloth in my hand. Ethel gave me an uneasy look. I shook my head and tried to give her a reassuring smile.

Keep your mind on your work, Joan. All of a sudden, I was swept with longing to see Inspector Marks. I mean, I was swept with a more specific longing, other than the usual, every-day longing I had to see him. I remembered how we'd once talked over a table such as this, late at night; how he'd listened to me and given me that look that I'd never once had from another person, not even Verity, who knew me best in the world. Inspector Marks looked at me like – like – I couldn't describe it. All I knew was that when his eyes met mine in that way, it warmed me through like a long drink of brandy.

I began wiping the table with renewed fervour. I would write to him, I decided there and then. There was no harm in that, surely? I would write to him and tell him what had happened here and, perhaps, ask his advice? Or would that be too forward? *He's probably forgotten you even exist*. I frowned and wiped savagely at a particularly stubborn stain.

Mrs Weston came into the room. I looked up and saw her face was shut tight like a box. All thoughts of asking what the matter was left me.

"Joan—" she began and hesitated. Her hand went up to the lace collar on her dress, the only bit of decoration on unremitting black. She tried again. "Joan, the police are coming back. I believe they might have a few more questions for you."

In an earlier life, when I was younger and more inexperienced, I would have immediately started to

THE HIDDEN HOUSE MURDERS

worry that I'd done something wrong. I didn't feel that now. Instead, I felt – yes – a leap of excitement, almost anticipation.

I managed to keep my voice calm and unexcited. "What do you think they want to know?"

"I don't have the least idea, I'm afraid." Her eyes flickered as she said this and I was fairly sure she'd just told me a falsehood. "They'll be here within the hour. Is luncheon underway?"

I felt a little surge of pride when I could answer in the affirmative. "There's one thing I do need to know, Mrs Weston, on that front."

"Yes, Joan?"

"How many will be sitting down? I heard that Mr Harrison and Mr Bentham would be returning to Cambridge."

Mrs Weston hesitated again. I had the feeling that whatever she was going to tell me was going to be told with extreme reluctance. "They – I believe they're staying another night, after all."

"So, there will be five to dine?"

"Yes." A muscle flickered in her cheek and our eyes met. There was something in her gaze that tugged at me. Was she... Was she asking for my help?

I made up my mind. "Mrs Weston, is there... Is there something wrong?"

That tightly shut face wavered for a moment, and I could see she wanted to say something. But then Ethel came bustling through from the pantry with her arms full of carrots and potatoes and the moment was lost.

"No, Joan. Thank you for your concern." She regarded me for a moment longer, nodded, and then swept away. I turned back to the kitchen table, questions turning themselves over and over in my mind.

Chapter Thirteen

LUNCH WAS PREPARED AND SERVED. I set out the servants' rather more humble meal, and Ethel and I sat down to await the arrival of Verity, Andrew and Mrs Weston. Verity entered in a hurry and, when we were all seated, ate her food in a kind of hasty, absentminded fashion that was quite unlike her. As I thought it, she caught my eye across the table and jerked her eyebrows upwards. My own went up in recognition of the fact that she had something to tell me.

"What is it?" I hissed as she helped me carry the dirty plates into the scullery. Ethel wasn't there and I felt we could talk reasonably safely.

Verity looked tense, her dark auburn eyebrows pulled down into a frown. "I know why the police are coming back."

I caught her tension, aware of the thump of my heart. "Why?"

Verity began to stack plates by the sink, making a lot of clatter. She kept her voice low. "They know

now that it wasn't food poisoning, or mushroom poisoning, that made everyone ill."

I moved closer so I could hear her. "Well, I'd assumed that. So, what was it?"

Verity's dark blue eyes met mine. "It was arsenic poisoning."

I dropped a plate and we both jumped back to avoid the shower of sharp china shards. I wasn't quick enough and a tiny piece nicked me on the shin, tearing my stocking at the same time. "Ouch!"

"Are you all right?"

"I'm fine," I said impatiently, rubbing away the tiny bead of blood. I was annoyed about my stocking, but that was a minor consideration compared to what I'd just heard. "*Arsenic* poisoning?"

Verity nodded, her mouth pinched in.

"How do you know this?" I asked.

"Dorothy told me. She spent almost an hour with Constable Palmer this morning. In fact, she wants you to go and see her when you can get away from the kitchen."

I fetched the dustpan and brush and began to clear up the broken plate, thinking fast. *Arsenic poisoning.* Well, that shone a whole new light on what had happened. I brushed all the pieces into the dustpan, barely seeing what I was doing. Could it have been accidental? Could arsenic somehow have contaminated the food that day? I shook my head impatiently at myself. Of course not; that was absurd. Suddenly, my mind was thronging with questions and I opened my mouth to ask Verity before realising that I should just go straight to Dorothy.

I got up from the floor and tipped the broken plate into the scrap pail. "Listen, V, I'll take Dorothy up some coffee or something. If Mrs Weston asks, can you tell her that?"

"Of course."

"I'll tell Ethel to carry on here." I began to set out a tray with a cup and saucer and reached for the kettle to re-boil it.

Verity was looking rather lost, as if she wanted to ask something but couldn't think of the words. As I put the finishing touches to Dorothy's tray, she began to say "Joan, do—" but then Ethel came scurrying back into the room and Verity snapped her mouth shut again.

"Thanks, V," I said. "Listen, we'll speak later."

She gave me a wan smile, a mere ghost of her usual marvellous grin, and slipped out. I picked up the coffee tray and began to make my way upstairs to Dorothy's bedroom.

When I knocked on the door, I expected to hear Dorothy's usual languid tone asking me to 'come in'. Instead, she opened the door to me herself, which shocked me slightly. What shocked me more was the look on her face. Dorothy looked, well, frightened – not an expression I was used to seeing on her face at all.

"Miss Drew?" I asked.

Anxiety gave way to impatience. "Oh, do come in, Joan. Don't just hover there on the doorstep."

I hurried in and Dorothy shut the door behind me. "I've brought you some coffee, Madam." Technically, Dorothy was a 'miss' but it always seemed a little impertinent to call her that.

"Thank you," she said vaguely. I will say that for Dorothy, she was always polite and well-mannered. It has obviously been bred into her from birth. "Put it down there on the table."

I did so and turned to face her, folding my hands before me. "You wanted to see me, Madam?"

Dorothy reached for her silver cigarette case and extracted one. "Want one, Joan? Oh no, you don't smoke, do you?" I wasn't shocked by her asking; she'd always been a bit odd like that. Dorothy gave away things like it was going out of fashion. It was partly why Verity was so well dressed. "Do sit down."

I perched myself on the edge of one of the easy chairs. Dorothy seated herself on the edge of the huge bed, one arm draped casually around one of the high brass bedposts. "Has Verity mentioned why I wanted to see you?" she asked.

I swallowed. Should I come out with it? "She said that you'd been speaking to Constable Palmer about – about—"

She gave me a wry look through a grey veil of smoke. "I *know* that Verity would have told you what we were talking about."

I gulped. "She said that the police think it was arsenic that made everyone so sick."

The smile fell from Dorothy's face. She looked, again, frightened. "Yes. That's what Constable Palmer told me." She took a last drag on her cigarette, looked about for an ashtray. I handed her one from the dressing table. "Oh, thanks. Yes. They decided to run some tests on poor Mrs Ashford because of – well, for a number of reasons really – but partly because of what you told Verity about the body being moved."

I nodded, listening but not commenting.

Dorothy went on. "Well, that clearly put the wind up them. So, they ran the tests and found arsenic in her stomach." She shuddered.

"Is that – Is that why she died?" I asked, wondering if I were being unfeeling by asking so bluntly.

Dorothy's face fell again. "No. She died of head injuries but she'd also had an almost lethal dose of arsenic as well." She lit another cigarette and I smothered a tiny cough. The air in the bedroom was blue with smoke already. "I got the impression that they don't actually know *exactly* what killed her. But that could be my interpretation." She looked up at me. "So, Joan, whatever happened, it looks as though it was a suspicious death."

I pinched my lips together and nodded, not sure of what to say.

Dorothy leant back on her elbows and blew smoke at the ceiling. I watched as her lit cigarette end got perilously close to the embroidered surface of the eiderdown and inwardly winced, but of course, it wasn't my place to say anything. Or should I? "Madam – Miss – your cigarette—"

Dorothy looked down, vaguely. "Oh, yes." She sat up again.

The silence in the room grew. I was on the verge of asking whether that was all when she spoke again, quite suddenly.

Dorothy sounded bitter. "I tell you, Joan, I sometimes feel as if I'm cursed."

What could I say? I knew what she meant. "I'm sorry to hear that, my lady."

Dorothy stared up at the writhing coils of smoke above her. "Cursed. Wherever I go, I can't seem to escape *death*." She flung herself back to a prone position again, uncaring of her cigarette, and stared fiercely ahead of her at nothing. "Sometimes I can't bear it."

The empty, exhausted tone of her voice worried me. "Should I get Verity for you, Madam? Can I get you anything?"

Dorothy took in a big gasp of smoke. "You can

get me a brandy, Joan. A big one. In fact, bring me up a bottle, if you can."

"Oh..." I felt three different things simultaneously; panic, guilt and sympathy. What the hell was I supposed to do? I couldn't refuse my mistress but she wasn't supposed to be drinking. *Oh, help...*

I took the coward's way out. "I'll – I'll go and see what I can do, Madam." I bobbed a curtsey and fled for the door.

"Wait." Dorothy's voice stopped me. I turned, hoping she'd changed her mind. She gestured to the writing desk over by the far wall. "Get me my writing paper, would you Joan? Before you go?"

I did so. Then I saw myself out and hurried off to find Verity, hoping against hope that she'd be able to sort out this mess better than I could myself.

Chapter Fourteen

HIDDEN HOUSE WASN'T PARTICULARLY BIG, as houses go, and one would have thought that I would have been able to track down Verity within a matter of minutes. I checked her bedroom, Dorothy's bathroom, and then hurried downstairs to look into the drawing room, the kitchen and the study. At least here, I could move freely about the house without anyone questioning my presence. I was rather startled to find Michael Harrison and Raymond Bentham playing billiards in the study, gramophone blasting out jazz. Luckily, the machine was making so much noise that my opening the door and exclaiming in shock went unnoticed, and they carried on bending over the billiard table with their cues, quite unaware of my presence. I quickly shut the door. Much as I needed to find Verity, seeing two of the house guests had reminded me that I really needed to get on with my work.

Oh, what on earth was I going to do about Dorothy? Should I take her the brandy? I was fairly sure that that would be a terrible idea but how could I refuse? Dorothy wasn't unreasonable, not normally, but she was under an enormous amount of strain (as were we all) and if she was gasping for a drink and I refused to give it to her, what would she do? She was well within her rights to dismiss me if I refused to carry out an order of hers. Oh, *help*... and where in damnation was Verity?

I found Mrs Weston in the linen cupboard, checking the sheets and towels. She looked up and caught sight of the look on my face. "Joan? What's wrong?" She looked frightened all of a sudden. "Are the police here again? Have they spoken to you?"

I'd almost forgotten that that's what she'd told me earlier that day. "No, Mrs Weston, I haven't seen them. I'm just looking for Verity."

"Is there something the matter?"

Curse my expressive face. "It's just Miss Drew is looking for her."

Mrs Weston looked relieved. "I believe Verity went into the village to run some errands. She should return shortly."

Damn it. What was I going to do about Dorothy's request for brandy? I thanked Mrs Weston and trailed back to the kitchen, thinking frantically. Ethel looked up from peeling potatoes.

"Mrs – Joan? Are you all right?"

I must have been muttering out loud. "I'm fine, Ethel, thank you." I caught sight of the bottle of cooking sherry that stood on the shelf by the range. That would have to do. I wasn't going to give Dorothy brandy, mistress of me, or not. I hunted out a sherry glass from the cabinet in the pantry, poured out a generous measure and carried it upstairs to Dorothy's room.

"I'm so sorry, Madam, but we seem to be out of brandy." I held the little glass of blood red liquid out before me like a peace offering. "I've brought you a sherry for...for your nerves."

For a moment, I thought Dorothy was going to be angry. Then, her innate sense of fairness and, perhaps, a little shame, made her give me a wry smile and hold out her hand for the glass. "Thank you, Joan. Send Verity up to me when you find her, will you?"

I bobbed, nodded and got myself out of the room. As I scurried off downstairs, I reflected on how much time I wasted on worrying myself half to death on things that never turned out to eventuate after all.

All the same, as Ethel and I began to plate up luncheon for the family and then for the servants, I thought about what I would say to Verity about Dorothy's request. Because I would have to say something. As I reflected, dumping spoonfuls of steaming stew onto plates, in an odd kind of way, Verity and I were the only real family that Dorothy now had. I wondered if Dorothy ever thought that herself. Probably not. The thought of an aristocratic lady being utterly emotionally reliant on a pair of servant girls would probably be the world's most horrifying thought. I drained the cabbage, turning my face from the cloud of rank steam that billowed up from the sink, and put all thoughts of our odd relationship away from me. Unlike Dorothy, I had a job to do.

I didn't even see Verity at luncheon. I was beginning to think the fairies had spirited her away. As Ethel and I set to the washing up, a shadow fell over the outside door and I looked up to see Verity coming in through the doorway looking purposeful.

"Joan, you do realise it's your afternoon off?" She said in a scolding tone. I gaped. I'd completely forgotten, given my worries about work, and Dorothy, and whether there was a poisoner at work amongst the household.

"Oh," I said, lamely. "Actually, I had forgotten." It seemed incredible, but the ways of this household were so much more relaxed than any of my previous places that free time didn't seem quite so important as it once had. Although, now that I realised Verity was right, I felt a leap of gladness at some time to myself.

"Come on," said Verity. "I've got a little picnic here. We can go for a walk and enjoy the sunshine by the river."

I flashed her a grateful look as I whipped off

my apron and hung it up. Giving Ethel some last minute instructions (I wasn't too worried – dinner plans were well underway and all she had to do was make sure it was served hot and on time), I attended to my untidy hair in the hallway mirror, pinched my cheeks and went to fetch my hat and coat.

WE DIDN'T SPEAK UNTIL WE were well away from the house, following a footpath through the forest. It was a beautiful spring day, and golden sunlight dappled the forest floor where the mist of early bluebells began to spread an azure carpet through the trees. The buds on the branches were gently unfurling in that special fresh green that lasts so little time before darkening.

"Phew," Verity said, tipping back her hat. "It's good to get away, isn't it?"

"Haven't you been in the village all morning?"

Verity nodded. "Yes. Dorothy had me send a telegram." She looked over at me as if considering telling me something and then obviously thought better of it.

"What is it?"

"Never mind. You'll see."

"V—" I warned her.

Verity giggled, always a pretty sound. "You'll see, Joanie. That's all."

"Hmm." I had no idea why she was being so

mysterious but at that moment, we reached the edge of the forest and a beautiful sight was before our eyes. The river foamed in sparkling silver waves across smoothly rounded stones and ferns and flowers danced in the breeze on the riverbanks.

"How delightful!" I exclaimed.

"It's lovely here," Verity agreed. "I came across it the other day." She gestured to a couple of large boulders by the edge of the bank. "We could sit there."

The rocks had been warmed by the sun. We sat there in silence for a moment, watching the little wavelets breaking over the riverbed stones. A fish leapt and splashed in a shining momentary streak of silver.

I could feel the tension in my shoulders ebb away as I watched the rippling water. Even so, I knew I should mention Dorothy's request for brandy to Verity. I did so and braced myself for her anger.

It didn't come. Instead she sighed and said "Well, she's been doing so well so far. I can understand why she might – might slip now."

This seemed as good a time as any to mention what I'd been thinking. "Who in the family would have wanted Mrs Ashford's death?"

Verity looked a little startled at my bluntness. She turned to stare at the river once more. "I don't know," was all she said, after a long moment's silence. I could see her forehead creasing into a frown.

"Is there something you're not telling me?" I asked, after a moment.

Verity didn't look at me. After a second, she muttered, "The police have been asking Mrs Weston about the arsenic. About whether she kept any in the house."

"Oh." I considered that for a moment, remembering the tension I had seen in Mrs Weston's face. "What did she say?"

"She said she couldn't say for sure but she didn't think they kept any arsenic." Verity pushed a wisp of hair away from her face. "Arabella apparently told the police that there was some cyanide in the garden shed because the gardener used it for getting rid of wasps."

"But Mrs Ashford didn't die of cyanide poisoning, did she?"

"No."

We were both silent for a moment. "Could it have been a mistake?" I muttered, almost to myself.

"What's that, Joanie?"

"The poisoning. Could it have been accidental?"

Verity looked unconvinced. "I don't see how."

"No, I suppose not." I remembered something Inspector Marks had once told me and added, "Apparently, if you soak fly-papers, you can get arsenic that way. Are there any fly-papers here?"

Verity shrugged. "I don't know. Probably."

We sat in silence for a few moments longer. Then, because I could no longer keep it inside myself, I asked "Do you not want to talk about this, V? Is that it?"

Verity didn't answer. Then she sighed and turned to face me. "Joan. I know that you – you *enjoy* this. I don't mean that in a macabre way," she added, when she saw I was about to protest. "But you do enjoy it. You like finding things out and working out puzzles and mysteries. And you're not scared, that's the thing. You're not scared of all this death and all this – this wickedness."

I was so flabbergasted for a moment that I couldn't respond. Verity, sensing that, pressed on. "I'm not like that. Oh, I know it was fun, to start with. At Asharton Manor. But we weren't really close to it there, or at least I wasn't. It was like...play acting. It didn't seem real and so it didn't scare me."

She fell silent. By now I'd recovered my tongue. "So, what are you saying, V?"

Verity looked as though she hadn't heard me. There was an urgency, a passion to her voice that I hadn't heard before. "Joan, I hate it. I hate being around all this – this *malevolence*. My mind doesn't work like yours; I can't see things like you do. It's like I'm blind and flailing around in the dark, and the only person who can stop me from falling down a deep hole, a hole I can't see, is you." She was quiet for a moment and then added, softly, "And that scares me."

I really didn't know what she meant by that and said so. Verity sighed.

"It's just...we won't always be working together," she said. "Not always. Life moves on and perhaps so shall we."

Now *I* was scared. "What do you mean?"

"I mean, sometime in the future, perhaps we won't be maids any more. We'll be married, or working in something different..."

I thought of the play that I'd finally finished, the manuscript locked away in the suitcase on my wardrobe. Would I ever have the courage to send it off to anyone – a director, or a producer, or even an actor? What was Verity doing, saying I was brave? Was she mad? I was the scarediest cat I knew.

I thought all of that in a second but all I said was, "Well, I hope you're right, V. But we'll still be friends, won't we?" Sudden terror gripped me by the throat. "Won't we?"

Verity took my hand. "Of *course* we will, you noodle. That's not in question." I clasped her hand in mine, more relieved than I could say.

On impulse, I decided to share my secret. "V...do you remember, I told you I was writing a play? You probably don't remember."

Verity looked at me in amazement. "Of course I do. I could hear you sometimes, bashing away on that old typewriter of Dorothy's. And you mean to say you've finished it? Oh, congratulations, Joanie! That's marvellous."

Of course, now that it was out there, I felt like dismissing it as nothing. "It's silly really, I'm sure it's no good at all—"

"Don't be ridiculous, of course it'll be good. You always had a way with words." I half-shrugged, pleased but embarrassed. "Anyway, more importantly, what are you going to do with it?"

"I don't know," I said, honestly. "I really don't know."

"Where is it? In your room?"

Where else would it be? I nodded. "I keep it in the suitcase on top of my wardrobe."

"You should send it off to a producer. Tommy might know just the chap. Oh, Joan, please do that. I'm sure you could find someone who was interested."

Now I felt more than embarrassment – I felt extreme reluctance. The thought of anyone else reading my words and judging them almost made me break out in a cold sweat, despite the warm sunshine. "Oh no, V – no, I couldn't. I just couldn't—"

"You *must*, Joan. Go on. Be brave."

"I can't," I said, with more finality. "Perhaps one day. But not right now. I just can't."

Verity looked stubborn, as if she'd like to say more. But I shook my head at her, smiling but in a definite *this conversation is over* way. She set her mouth but shut up.

We sat in slightly uncomfortable silence for a moment or two.

Verity tipped her face back to the sun. "Well, you can do what you think best Joan. But I tell you, I'm not going to be a lady's maid for the rest of my life. I want *more*. And I can't have more if – if I keep getting caught up in murder. It's too dangerous."

I was silent. I knew what she was saying was true. It was just that I didn't feel like that myself. Oh, of course, I knew that there was danger, but I never felt as if I would be affected by it. Perhaps that was royally foolish of me, given the near misses I'd had in the past. I thought of Merisham Lodge and what had happened in the kitchen there and my hand flew to my throat before I could think about stopping it.

Verity gave me a keen look. "I *know* you know what I mean."

I sighed. "I do. It's just – oh...I can't describe it. It's almost as if...as if this is what I'm *meant* to do. I mean, if fate hadn't meant me to do this, why do I keep getting mixed up in all these strange happenings?"

Now Verity did grin. "Don't ask me, Joanie. You're just a magnet for murder!"

That struck both of us as funny, God knows why, but we laughed. When our giggles tapered off, we were silent again for a long moment, watching the splash and sparkle of the river.

"Come on," Verity said eventually. "Let's have our picnic."

I found myself to be quite hungry, which was surprising given that I'd not long had lunch. It must have been the fresh air. We set to with a will and the rest of the afternoon passed in pleasant conversation and a stroll along the riverbank. Thoughts of murder and mayhem may have been on our minds, but they weren't mentioned again.

Chapter Fifteen

I ROSE THE NEXT MORNING IN a thoughtful mood. As I washed and pinned up my hair under my cap, and tried to make myself look semi-respectable (not always an easy task), I was thinking about what Verity and I had talked about the day before. I should have been looking back on our sunny afternoon with pleasure, and I was, but it was tinged with disquiet. I hadn't realised Verity felt that way about our – well, it was hard to know how to term them. Our pursuit of justice? Our crime-fighting escapades?

The last was so ridiculous that it made me laugh, even as I pulled on my shoes, washed my hands and walked downstairs to the kitchen. *Put it out of your mind, Joan.* I had a busy day ahead of me, with no time to waste on what the future might hold. It was another beautiful day, golden and sunny, the tightly curled buds on the trees now unfolding and the spring flowers out in all their delicate, colourful finery.

I was hard at work, trying to assemble a tricky

bouillabaisse for the dinner that evening when a shadow fell over the kitchen door. Concentrating on what I was doing, I scarcely noticed until a deep, masculine voice, a well-remembered voice, said something, and I looked up and gasped, a fish-head falling from my fingers.

"Good morning, Miss Hart," Inspector Marks said, smiling. He was just as handsome and dapper as I remembered, his black hair and moustache neatly trimmed, a trilby set square on his head. His suit looked to be a rather better one than I remembered him wearing before. Mind you, I was so taken aback, he could have come in wearing a Scotsman's kilt and it wouldn't have thrown me more.

I gaped like a goldfish for a good few seconds too long before reason returned and I straightened up sharply, wiping my fishy hand on my apron. My second thought, after the first shock of seeing him, was that he *would* have had to come and see me while I was making fish stew. The kitchen and everything in it, including me, stank of fish. Instinctively, my hands went up to my hair, checking for wisps before I forced them down again, not wanting to make matters worse.

"Inspector Marks," I said eventually, trying to regain my composure. "What a surprise."

The inspector looked surprised himself. "You didn't realise I was coming?"

Would I look like this if I had? was what I *didn't* say.
I shook my head. "No, I—" Belatedly, I remembered
Verity telling me to expect a surprise. And giggling
while she said it. The little *minx*. She knew some of
my feelings about the inspector although not the
innermost, secret workings of my heart. Cheeks
burning, I tried to pull myself together. "No, I didn't
know at all. It's – it's a pleasure to see you, sir."

I had almost forgotten Ethel was in the room.
I caught sight of her, goggling like a little child at
a Punch and Judy show and almost giggled myself.
"Could I make you a cup of tea or something, sir?"

"Yes please, Miss Hart." Had he forgotten that
he'd once called me Joan? I felt a thump of the heart
but smiled bravely. "In fact, I'd like us to sit down
and have a – a conference, I suppose you'd call it.
Would that be possible?"

My heart began to thump even louder. "Yes. Yes
of course. Ethel—" I struggled momentarily with
my conscience in leaving my inexperienced kitchen
maid to the difficult dish I was in the middle of
making and then threw caution to the wind. "Ethel,
could you carry on with what I was doing here? It's
quite easy—" *God forgive me.* "Well, *fairly* easy. Just
consult the recipe book and do your best. I won't be
long."

Would I? I had a pretty shrewd idea of what
Inspector Marks wanted to ask me, although I could
have been wrong. Ethel was still looking at the

inspector with her mouth hanging open. Resisting the temptation to close it with my finger, I tapped the relevant page of the recipe book and took off my apron.

Inspector Marks came a little closer as I was washing my hands at the sink. "Is there somewhere we can talk privately, Miss Hart?"

He was near enough for me to smell his cologne. I felt my face heat up again. Unfortunately, he was probably near enough to smell the *eau de haddock* on me. What I would have given for one of Dorothy's expensive French perfumes right then... "There's a small sun terrace outside," I said. "It's a lovely morning and we shouldn't be—" I stopped abruptly, aware of Ethel listening to every word. I had been going to say *we shouldn't be overheard*.

"Ethel, could you bring us some tea please?" I asked with an encouraging smile. Then, quaking a little, I led Inspector Marks outside and round to the terrace.

WHEN WE SAT FACING ONE another on separate wooden benches, I was struck afresh by how unreal the whole situation seemed. Was this *really* Inspector Marks sitting opposite me? I blinked a few times in the bright sunlight, wondering if I were dreaming.

"Well, Miss Hart," said the inspector, smiling. "Here we are again."

I shook myself back to reality. "It's very nice to see you, sir." The second I said it, I wondered whether I'd been too bold. But it really *was* very nice to see him.

We regarded each other for a moment longer. "Here you are again, mixed up in murder," Inspector Marks said eventually.

"It's not as if I *planned* it," I said, indignation making my voice rise.

The inspector grinned, teeth flashing white under his black moustache. "No, you just seem to have a kind of...genius for getting yourself into these situations." He rasped a hand along his jaw for a moment, considering. "A flair, perhaps."

I wasn't sure whether to feel complimented or insulted. Just as I was wondering what to say, the inspector suddenly became brisk. "Anyway, Miss Hart, I need your help."

I sat up myself. "I'll help in any way I can, sir."

"I knew I could rely on you."

He began to say something else and then, at the chime of crockery and Ethel's heavy footsteps behind us, obviously decided against it. I took the tray from Ethel's hands and gave her a grateful but dismissive smile.

Once she was out of earshot, I sat back down and poured the tea, looking (I hoped) alertly at

Inspector Marks. What was his Christian name? It had never occurred to me before to wonder but now I wanted to know. I didn't see how I could be quite so bold as to ask him, though.

"Joan, you probably know that the police are now treating the death of Mrs Ashford as murder."

"Yes." I handed him a cup. There was obviously more to come.

"Thank you. Obviously, I can't share everything I know with you but one particular fact is about to become common knowledge."

"Was it arsenic poisoning that she died of, sir?"

Inspector Marks took a sip of tea. "Well, unfortunately it's impossible to say whether she died from poisoning or from a head injury. The dose of arsenic she was given was...shall we say, *fairly* unlikely to have caused the death of a young, healthy person, but Mrs Ashford was old and frail. Unless one is a trained chemist, it's not an exact science anyway – I mean, working out what would be a lethal dose."

We were still sitting in bright sunlight but the light seemed to dim a little. I looked at the shimmering brown surface of my teacup and repressed a shudder.

Inspector Marks went on. "Now, again, the head injury *could* have been accidental. The attending doctor was at first completely convinced that she'd had a fall."

"Yes, he did think that. So did I, at first, when

I saw her body. I thought she'd got up out of bed for whatever reason, tripped and fallen onto the hearthstone."

"You saw the body? Oh yes, of course you did. You were the one who told PC Palmer it had been moved."

Honesty compelled me to answer. "Well, I didn't know that for certain but...it seemed odd. I just had an odd feeling that something wasn't quite right."

Inspector Marks gave me a wry look. "Well, I know you've seen a few bodies, Miss Hart. Not as many as me, but enough."

I smiled back. "That was why I took some time to mention it to anyone. I thought perhaps my – my past experience was colouring my view here."

"Not in this instance." The inspector leaned forward. "Now, take me through exactly what happened."

"From finding the body?"

"From when you arrived at this house. If you have the time."

I probably didn't have the time but, right at that moment, I didn't care. I could have sat in that sunlit garden, drinking tea with Inspector Marks, all day, and if he wanted to talk of murder and poison and motives for killing, then that was fine with me.

I sat up a little straighter in my chair. "Well, sir, Verity and I – you remember my friend, Miss Hunter – we arrived on the twenty-seventh of March, I think it was the twenty-seventh and we were collected from the station..."

Chapter Sixteen

I COULDN'T WAIT UNTIL THAT EVENING to talk to Verity alone. When we sat down to dinner, I found her foot under the table, pressed it hard – perhaps harder than necessary – and waited for her to look at me. When she did, I signalled as hard as I could without moving my face that I needed to talk to her *immediately*.

She got the unspoken message. Verity and I had known each other for so long and had had to communicate without words so often that it sometimes felt as if we could almost read each other's minds. I could tell, looking at her across the table, that she was feeling both sheepish, a little guilty but also gleefully triumphant and I knew why.

After dinner, I sent Ethel to begin to clear the family dining room and, once Mrs Weston was out of the way, virtually pushed Verity into the scullery.

"You – you cat, you!"

Verity burst out laughing. "I thought you'd appreciate the surprise."

I couldn't help but laugh myself. "Honestly, V, you might have given me *some* warning. I looked like something that had been dragged through a hedge backwards when the inspector arrived."

That made Verity laugh harder. "It's not as if he doesn't know what you do, Joanie. He knows you're a cook, not a...a policewoman or a – what was the other alter-ego of yours? A journalist?"

I almost blushed to think of some of the folly I'd made up in the past. "Well, I would have still appreciated a bit of warning."

Verity suppressed her giggles with an effort. "Sorry," she said with dancing eyes, not sounding it in the slightest.

"Well!" I said, not quite sure of what else to say.

Verity sobered up. "What did he actually want? Dorothy said he wanted to talk to you before he would talk to her. I think she was a bit cross about that."

I felt a mixture of pride and anxiety. "Well, Dorothy was the one who wrote to him, I suppose. But she wrote to him because of what I knew."

"I know that. Don't worry about it, anyway. She'll get over it." We both simultaneously became aware of footsteps approaching the kitchen and exchanged a wordless glance.

"Thanks for your help, Verity," I said loudly, pushing open the scullery door.

"You're very welcome, Joan," Verity said, equally

clearly. As she passed me, she murmured "My room, when we're finished." I nodded in agreement and watched her walk past Mrs Weston and Ethel who were both carrying trays of dirty dishes.

BECAUSE I WAS DYING TO continue our conversation, of course everything conspired against me. Mrs Weston wanted to discuss the menus for the week, not just the next day, which took ages. She looked rather unwell, pale-faced and hollow-eyed, and once or twice she stopped talking and pressed a hand to her forehead. It was on the tip of my tongue to ask her if she was feeling ill but the moment I essayed the most tentative enquiry, she snapped that she was perfectly well and so I held my tongue for the rest of our discussion.

Eventually, once the dishes were washed, the kitchen was tidy and prepared for the morning, Ethel had been dismissed and the back door locked, I made my weary way upstairs. Ethel was in the bathroom, so that gave me the perfect excuse to quietly knock on Verity's bedroom door and slip inside.

VERITY'S ROOM WAS SUCH A contrast to my own. Originally, it had had the same austere furnishings as mine, but she had added ornaments and hung clothes about and brought in a beautiful spring bouquet of flowers that looked wonderful despite their vase being a chipped earthenware pot. Verity could sew wonderfully well and she'd made a perfectly lovely bedspread for her bed, embroidered all over with little birds and rosebuds and green leaves. It was almost like a lady's bedroom, and I vowed once more, as I always did after a visit, that I would do something more with my own little room. Why, the only precious thing I had in my room that was mine was my play.

Verity sat brushing her fox-fur hair out in front of the mirror and she caught my eye in the reflection and smiled and turned around, putting down the brush. I flopped down onto her bed, fighting the urge to curl up and go to sleep there.

"Did Dorothy say anything else about Inspector Marks?" I asked. I was curious, of course, but weariness was beginning to tell. I had a fleeting thought that, if I wasn't quite so fatigued all the time, I would have been able to solve this case by now. Then I grinned at myself. Solve the case! As if I were a real detective or something.

"She said he wanted to know everything she could tell him about everyone. A real run down of the family and the guests."

"Well, he certainly went to the right person," I said drily.

Verity giggled. "And she said he wants to talk to you again."

Tired as I was, I felt a leap of the heart. "Oh," was all I said, my heart beating faster.

Verity grinned, not fooled by my casual tone. "So, you'd best not cook anything too disgusting tomorrow."

"Do you *mind*? My cooking is never disgusting."

"No, of course it's not, Joanie. I'm sorry." Verity got up, stretched and yawned. "Oh my, I'm so sleepy."

I forced myself up. "I'll let you get to bed."

"It's fine—" Her yawn belied her words and I caught it. "Oh, there was something else."

"Oh yes?"

Verity climbed into bed and I tucked the counterpane over her feet. "Oh, thanks Joanie. Gosh, it's nice to have someone fussing over me for a change."

I knew how she felt. The cups of tea that Ethel made me tasted so much sweeter than the ones I made myself. "What was it you were going to tell me?"

"Oh yes. It's – Mrs Ashford's will is going to be read tomorrow."

I was silent. Again, I was suddenly convinced that the piece of paper Verity and I had signed had been a will. Perhaps the one being read tomorrow. I chewed my lip, thinking.

"Mr Brittain – that's Mrs Ashford's solicitor – is coming tomorrow, late morning." Verity yawned again and wriggled down under the covers.

"I wish I could hear it." I moved over to let her push her feet past me. "But I don't see how I can." I looked at her pale face on the pillow, her eyes almost closing. "I don't suppose you could?"

She yawned again. "I'll try. I can't promise. It completely depends on what Dorothy wants to do."

"I understand." Taking pity on her, I patted the bulge of her feet under the covers and got up. "Get some sleep, V. I'll think of something."

"Night-night." Her voice flattened out to a sleepy mumble. Smiling, I turned off the bedside light for her and tiptoed over to the doorway in the dark.

Chapter Seventeen

SURPRISINGLY I SLEPT WELL AND didn't dream, despite all the muddle and tension and worry of the present. I opened my eyes to bright sunlight, which always helped my mood. As Ethel and I prepared breakfast, I sent up a mental message of thanks to Verity for her tip-off about the solicitor, Mr Brittain, coming to read Mrs Ashford's will that morning. That meant he would no doubt stay to luncheon, and I was able to draft out a suitable menu before Mrs Weston even set foot in the kitchen.

She looked far worse than she had the night before; so ill, in fact, that I was unable to help commenting. "Mrs Weston, are you quite well?"

She shook her head. "Joan, Ethel, I must take to my bed for a little while." We both tried to say something but she held up a trembling hand. "Please, don't be alarmed. I don't believe it's food poisoning again." I bit my lip. Surely, she wasn't still clinging to the false hope that it had been the food that had made everyone ill and killed her mistress?

"I... I believe I have influenza. Joan, I need you to assist me today. Do you know Mr Brittain is coming to the house this morning?"

I nodded. "Yes, and I understood he would be staying for luncheon?"

"Yes. That's right." Mrs Weston's face was sheeny with sweat.

"Please don't worry, Mrs Weston, I've already planned the meal. And I can hold the fort so you can get some rest."

"They will need refreshments in the drawing room when Mr Brittain arrives. Please make sure there's sufficient seating and stay in the room in case anyone is in need of assistance."

I kept my face steady and nodded but felt a leap of excitement. I'd been wondering how I could find out what was in Mrs Ashford's will and here was the perfect opportunity. "Of course, Mrs Weston."

"Thank you, Joan." She looked as though she wanted to continue issuing instructions but a fresh layer of sweat broke out on her forehead. "Oh dear, I must lie down."

"Let me help you," I said, hating to think of her struggling up the stairs alone. She was too weak to give me more than a token protest.

I saw her up to her room and laid down on her bed, and I made sure she had water and an extra blanket nearby. Then I went to leave. I was almost at the door when her voice stopped me.

"Thank you, Joan."

"That's quite all right, Mrs Weston."

She settled her head back on the pillow and smiled, the first real smile I'd ever received from her. "I'm beginning to realise why Miss Drew didn't want to lose you."

That remark bore me down two flights of steps with a warm feeling in my chest. It was good to think that I was valued, that my hard work was recognised. I realised that was partly why I felt so drawn to Inspector Marks. I felt he really saw me as a person. He respected my opinions. He appreciated my...my skills. Because I had had some success in this strange sort of business, hadn't I? For the first time then, my foot upon the top step of the lower flight of stairs, I realised it. I was *good* at this. At investigating crime. Perhaps it was the way my mind worked. Perhaps it was intuition. Honesty compelled me to add to myself that perhaps it was luck. Smiling to myself, I went back downstairs to the kitchen.

Mr Brittain arrived promptly at eleven and I showed him to the drawing room, standing in for Mrs Weston as she'd requested. The others were gathered there already. Mrs Bartleby stood by the window, her hand to her throat, fiddling with a string of jet beads. She was dressed in deepest mourning. Everybody else wore black, or sombre shades, save for Raymond Bentham who, shockingly, wasn't even wearing a tie. His white shirt gaped open and I could see Arabella casting sideways glances at the small triangle of brown skin revealed there. Not completely overtaken by grief then, I observed silently to myself with an inner grin. Then I told myself not to be so judgemental.

Michael and Dorothy sat together on the chaise longue, conversing quietly with each other. I could see Mrs Bartleby giving them rather puzzled covert glances and took a closer look myself. With a twinge of unease, I could see that there was a new sort of intimacy to their posture, their heads together, leaning in towards one another. Michael was assiduous in lighting Dorothy's cigarette. Oh well, no doubt she knew what she was doing, and it wasn't as if he weren't charming, handsome and a gentleman. But he was rather younger than she and I didn't know what his prospects were. *Hark at you, you sound like her mother, Joan.* Dorothy was rich enough, anyway. Really, aside from the social aspect, she could marry who she liked. I dismissed the thought and turned my attention to arranging the refreshments on the sideboard. Then I stood back against the wall unobtrusively and folded my hands in front of me.

Mr Brittain was a tall, rather stooped old man with bushy white eyebrows and an equally luxuriant moustache. He cleared his throat and walked to the front of the room. Every conversation ceased and every eye, including my own, turned to look at him.

"Good morning, everybody, and may I first express my deepest condolences to you, Miss Arabella, and indeed you all, at this very sad time." He looked at Arabella with stern pity; she smiled tremulously and shifted ever so slightly in her chair. "As you no doubt know, I am here in my capacity as the late Mrs Margaret Ashford's solicitor and will shortly read her last will and testament."

He continued with a fairly lengthy testimony as to Mrs Ashford's 'strength of character', 'high moral sense' and 'astute and frugal ways'. I had never actually been to a will reading before, so perhaps this was the usual practice, but I could sense a tiny shift in the concentration of those people raptly listening as he droned on. There were small corrections of posture, coughs and glances at pocket watches and the clock on the mantelpiece. Raymond looked frankly bored, and I wondered if he'd get up and walk out. It wasn't likely that he'd been left anything, was it? But he stayed put, one ankle crossed on his knee. Arabella had taken the seat directly next to his, of course. I was conscious of a spurt of pity for her.

At long last, Mr Brittain came to the point. "The estate of my late client is quite substantial, consisting of this house, the land surrounding it and a sum in the region of fifty thousand pounds."

I saw Arabella's shoulders tense as she sat forward slightly. "As it happens, the estate will be divided as so. Miss Arabella Jane Ashford will inherit the house and the land. The remainder of the estate, held in a mixture of cash, stocks and shares and government bonds, will be divided equally between Miss Arabella Jane Ashford and Mrs Constance Mary Bartleby. A legacy of five thousand pounds will be given to Mr Michael Harrison—"

He went on to detail various small legacies to people such as Dorothy and Mrs Weston, and several cousins and nieces and nephews, but I was no longer listening because I was watching the reactions of various people. Really, I thought, a will reading is better than the theatre. I watched Arabella jerk and then relax, sinking back into her chair, that tremulous smile growing stronger. I heard Mrs Bartleby's gasp but couldn't tell if it was delight or shock or horror. Michael Harrison caught Dorothy's eye and smiled a rueful yet resigned smile. Raymond looked as though he were thinking about nothing, or possibly about his dinner.

I had left Ethel with strict instructions for the dinner – or rather, the luncheon – but I felt a qualm of anxiety as to how it was progressing. Mrs Weston's orders or no, I decided I would have to go downstairs to make sure everything was in order. Mr Brittain had finished reading by now and was engaged in polishing his silver-rimmed spectacles.

The room seethed with a variety of emotions, and I badly wanted to stay and see what was going to happen. I battled with my conscience for a moment and then duty prevailed. Also, from the view of my own self-preservation, I didn't want this emotional group to be annoyed further by a bad meal.

I slipped out of the room just as people were beginning to pick themselves up out of their chairs and prepare to move. I had my hand on the rail of the basement staircase when there was a rustle and swish of black silk behind me and Mrs Bartleby's voice snapped. "Where is Mrs Weston?" The anger vibrating through her normally low and charming voice disturbed me.

"She's – I'm afraid she's unwell, Madam. She's lying down in her room."

Mrs Bartleby said nothing in response but huffed in what I assumed was outrage and then turned about and went towards the stairs. I stared after her as she climbed the staircase quickly, heels thudding on the treads, even over the carpet runner that flowed down the middle of the staircase. Then, casting duty and caution to the wind, I followed her, far enough behind so that she didn't notice me doing so. Quickly, I snatched a newspaper from the sideboard in the hallway as I went past. If challenged, I could say I was delivering it to somebody's room.

As I crept along the corridor to the second set of

stairs, I saw Mrs Bartleby's long skirts whisk around the corner of the staircase. Now on uncarpeted wood, her heels sounded like gunshots on the boards. She was clearly very angry about something but what? I thought back to what I'd just heard in the drawing room. Surely it couldn't be over her inheritance? It sounded, from what I'd understood, that Mrs Ashford's estate was quite substantial and she, Mrs Bartleby, had inherited a significant portion of it. I slowed my pace, not wanting her to see my lurking at the bottom of the stairs. I heard the bedroom door open upstairs – she didn't knock – and her voice asking crossly "Mrs Weston? Mrs Weston?"

I took a deep breath and slowly crept up a few more of the stairs, enough to hear a little clearer. I could hear Mrs Weston's voice, sounding – as well it might – rather weary and flat. Mrs Bartleby seemed to be taking her to task about something failing to be posted.

"You assured me that everything was in hand, Mrs Weston – you gave me your assurance."

"I'm very sorry, Mrs Bartleby, but it was Mrs Ashford who asked me not to – not to post it. I couldn't disobey her wishes."

"I don't believe it for a second." Scorn reverberated in Mrs Bartleby's voice. "You had the *presumption* to think that you knew better than your very mistress – who, I might remind you, had *just* come

154

to the same conclusion that we all had and knew what she was doing was for the best—"

"I'm sorry, Mrs Bartleby, but she had changed her mind—"

"Nonsense. Absolute nonsense. I can tell you now, Mrs Weston, that I am most seriously displeased—"

Voices swelled in the hallway beneath me and I reluctantly moved away, back to the corridor. I really had to get back to the kitchen or risk a complete culinary disaster. As I scurried back downstairs, I was conscious of a spurt of anger towards Mrs Bartleby. Whatever Mrs Weston had or hadn't done, there was something distasteful in not even being able to be indisposed without one of the family chastising you. In your *bed*, no less.

I paused on the main staircase as everyone, bar Mrs Bartleby, flooded out of the drawing room and dispersed to various parts of the house. Michael and Raymond peeled off to the library, no doubt to drink whisky and play billiards. I heard Michael talking as they passed. "Frightfully good of the old girl, Ray, what? I wasn't expecting to get a bean after – well, after all that's happened."

I saw Arabella flinch a little at this as she and Dorothy walked past. Seconds later, it was as if her temporary discomfort was forgotten. If it wasn't for the fact that her mother had just died in suspicious circumstances, I would have said that she looked happy.

"You two chaps aren't going to moulder indoors on a day like this, are you?" Dorothy enquired of the young men. "How about a game of tennis after lunch?" She looked up and caught my eye. "Oh, Joan. When are we having grub?"

"Within the hour, Madam," I said, hoping that I wasn't inadvertently lying. I really had to get back to the kitchen.

"Jolly good."

"Join us for a pre-luncheon snifter, eh?" Michael smiled at the women. "Toast my good fortune – and yours too, Arabella." She looked at him quite warily before she smiled, uncertainly. "And we must raise a glass to my dear, late aunt, of course."

"What a good idea," Dorothy said, with a lot more enthusiasm than I would have liked. I watched the four of them disappear towards the library and sighed, wondering if I should warn Verity. But there wasn't much that she could do, really, was there?

Mr Brittain emerged last from the drawing room and looked around, as if surprised to be alone. Before he could ask me anything, Mrs Bartleby came stalking down the staircase and swept past me as if I weren't there. She had a hard smile on her face that might have fooled you, if you hadn't just been party to what she'd been saying to Mrs Weston.

"Oh, Mr Brittain, do come and have a sherry before luncheon."

"Well, Mrs Bartleby, that would be very kind..."

I watched them walk back into the drawing room and then pelted for the kitchen, hoping against hope that Ethel had everything under control.

Chapter Eighteen

As it turned out, I was worrying for nothing. Ethel – the good girl – had the pots bubbling and the plates heating. I could simply whisk in, make a few last-minute adjustments and begin dishing everything up.

Once the family's meal was underway, I prepared one for the servants. What with Mrs Weston being out of the way, they could sit down to a cold meal for once; cold meats, cheese, bread and some of the chutneys that had been made here last year. I made up a tray for the invalid and Ethel carried it up.

After we washed up, I said, "Ethel, you did marvellously this morning. Thank you. If you wish, you're welcome to have the next couple of hours off. I can manage dinner."

Of course she wished to. I didn't blame her. Much as I honestly wanted to reward her, I also wanted her out of the way for the afternoon. I had to talk to Verity and – if I could manage it – I had to talk to Inspector Marks.

Verity was easy. I found her coming out of the study with an empty whisky bottle in her hand and a grim look on her face.

"What's the matter?" I asked in a low voice, although the hubbub behind the study door meant I was in little danger of being overheard.

"What do you think?" She waved the empty bottle at me.

"Oh, V. There's nothing you can do—"

"I *know* that. It's just... It's frustrating."

Selfishly, for I could see she was worried, I realised that if Dorothy was on the toot for the next hour or so, that meant I could have Verity's undivided attention. "Come downstairs for a cup of tea," I suggested. "Have a little rest for a while. Dorothy will be fine. She's a... She's a big girl."

Verity rolled her eyes but she didn't protest. I made tea and took it out to the little terrace out the back where I'd sat with Inspector Marks. He was staying at the inn in the village, I remembered him telling me. If I had time later, I would telephone him there and leave a message if he wasn't there to receive my call.

I let Verity talk about Dorothy for a bit as I could see that if she didn't, she was going to explode.

"I thought she was doing so well and being here seemed to be just the thing. Arabella's not really one for cocktails – she's not very *gay*, at all really, in any way, is she? Dorothy was doing so well, and then these two young men arrive and it's straight back into bad habits..."

"Are Dorothy and Michael... Er...?" I asked, curious, and thinking that a change of subject might be a good thing.

"Are they 'er'?" To her credit, Verity stopped ranting and laughed. "They might be. He is awfully handsome, isn't he? And Dorothy's always had an eye for a good-looking man." She sighed, and added "Perhaps I should encourage it. It might take her mind off the demon drink."

"Didn't he once have an *amour* with Arabella?" I said this merely to keep Verity off the subject of Dorothy's intoxication.

"Well, I think that's what Mrs Ashford would have liked, but it didn't work out. I think Michael was a bit keener than she was."

"And now she's falling over herself to get Raymond Bentham."

Verity re-filled her cup. "Well, she might have a bit more of a chance with him now she's an heiress."

"Surely that can't be very nice, knowing that someone's only with you because of your money?"

Verity turned her face up into the sunlight. "Gosh, this sun is lovely. I could stay out here all day. What was that, Joan?" I repeated what I had just said. "Oh, well, chance would be a fine thing for us, wouldn't it?" I giggled ruefully. "Oh, who knows why anyone does anything? I don't know anymore."

She sounded more defeated than I would have liked. I hesitated, wondering whether to bring the next subject up or not.

"Um, Verity?"

"Mm?" Her eyes were closed, face tipped up to the sky.

"Do you remember that – that paper we signed, the first night we arrived here?"

Verity kept her eyes shut. "What? Oh, that. Yes, what about it?"

I recounted the strange conversation – argument, really – that I'd overheard between Mrs Bartleby and Mrs Weston. "I think it was a will."

That snapped Verity's eyes open. "A will? What, *the* will we heard read today?"

I paused. "Well, I don't know. But I don't see how it can have been. Not with the way Mrs Bartleby was going on at Mrs Weston. What if it was a new will and Mrs Weston was supposed to post it and for some reason she didn't, and so the old will was read today?"

Verity frowned. "Tell me again what Mrs Bartleby said, Joan."

I cudgelled my memory and tried to repeat, word for word, what I'd overheard. *Eavesdropped*, said a little devilish voice and I batted it away. *Needs must when the devil drives.*

Verity frowned harder. "She said 'you think that

161

you knew better than your very mistress – who had just come to the same conclusion that we all had…'"

"Something like that." I tried to think back even further. "I overheard Arabella and her mother arguing over Raymond Bentham and her mother said something like 'there's only one thing I could do to change your mind'. I always wondered what she meant by that." I remembered that nasty laugh Mrs Ashford had given during that conversation and then, the flattened tone of Arabella belying the violence of her words. *I hate you.*

Verity reached for the teapot and made a noise of annoyance when she realised it was empty. "Well, *if* you're right about there being another will, and *if* you're right about it going missing, I still don't understand Mrs Bartleby's annoyance. She's just inherited twenty-five thousand pounds. That's a fortune, by anyone's standards."

I shook my head helplessly. "I know. I don't understand it either. Perhaps we've got it all completely wrong."

We looked at each other for a moment. Then Verity put the teapot back on the table with finality. "You need to talk to the inspector, Joan. Whether we've got things right or wrong, we need to tell him."

Although I had planned to do just that, I felt a keen pleasure at being given permission to talk to Inspector Marks by my friend. "Well, I suppose I should," I said, absurdly, as if I hadn't just been plotting and planning the telephone call I was next about to make.

Verity sighed. "Come on, we'd better go back. I need to see if Dorothy's still upright."

I squeezed her arm in sympathy. "You just come and find me if you...if you need help. Or Andrew." Verity gave me a grimace. Andrew, the footman and chauffeur, had already had some experience of decanting a comatose Dorothy from the back seat of her car to her bed. To be fair to him, though, he was discreet and never mocked her. Not to our faces, anyway.

As we walked back to the kitchen, another unwelcome thought came to me. "Oh."

Verity looked across as I stopped short. "Now what is it?"

I brushed aside the shortness of her tone. "I've just thought of something. About Mrs Bartleby." I lowered my voice. "You remember when Mrs Ashford died?"

"Yes." I could tell Verity was trying to keep the impatience out of her voice.

"Well, Mrs Bartleby was with her. With the body. In her room. Mrs Weston and I left her in there, alone."

Verity raised her coppery brows. "And?"

"Well..." I hesitated. "What if it was she who moved the body? To cover up what she'd done?"

Now it was Verity's turn to hesitate. "I suppose

it's possible," she said slowly. Then she seemed to shake herself and come back to reality. "Well, we can't spend all day discussing it. Talk to Inspector Marks." She gave me an assessing look and then her grin flashed out. "Not that *that* will be a hardship, eh, Joanie?"

I dug her in the ribs with my elbow, pursing my mouth in mock disapproval and we both snorted and walked back to the kitchen giggling.

Chapter Nineteen

ALL WAS QUIET IN THE kitchen when we returned. So quiet, in fact, that I could clearly hear the noise of the gramophone and the occasional loud laugh and shriek echoing from the study on the floor above. Verity caught my eye and rolled hers. I knew how she felt. Perhaps Mrs Ashford was not much missed but it did seem a trifle unseemly to be, well, *celebrating* the fact in such an overt manner. I hoped Mr Brittain had departed.

Verity disappeared upstairs with promises to come and get me if I was needed. I glanced around me at the quiet kitchen and fastened my apron around my waist once more. Then I took it off again. This would be the perfect time to telephone the inspector.

Talking on the telephone always flustered me a little, although you would have thought I'd have been used to it, given the amount of ordering I was expected to do with the tradesmen. The exchange connected me to the inspector's inn and I waited with my heart in my mouth for the receptionist to answer.

Glory be and hallelujah, the inspector was in his room. I waited, heart thumping ever more wildly, for him to pick up the receiver at his end.

"Miss Hart? What can I do for you?" Was it me, or could I truly ascertain a note of pleasure in his voice at hearing from me?

Succinctly as I could, I summarised the information I had to give him. "I would really like to talk to you, sir. I was wondering if we could meet?"

"You have the jump on me, Miss Hart. I was about to suggest the same thing."

I ignored the leap of excitement in my stomach and listened to his suggestion of a meeting in an hour or so. Just as I was about to comment, I heard something on the line that made me pause. A stealthy click which I recognised as someone picking up a telephone to listen in on the line.

I think the inspector heard it too. He merely reiterated his suggestion but there was a minute pause and a slight artificiality to his voice that made me think he was wondering if someone else was listening in.

He confirmed that he was on his way to the house and said goodbye. "Take good care of yourself, Miss Hart," he said, with slightly pointed emphasis on the words *take care*.

"I will, sir. Good bye."

I put the receiver down, wondering if I really had heard someone pick up the other line. And if I hadn't been mistaken, who had it been? Before I could hesitate and tell myself I'd been hearing things, I crept out from Mrs Weston's parlour, where the telephone was located and quickly but quietly hurried upstairs. The only other telephone was kept in the drawing room. I pressed myself against the wall of the hallway, around from where the drawing room door was situated, and waited. Sure enough, there was the click of heels and the sound of the door being opened. I held my breath. A swish of silk and the patter of feet as someone ran upstairs from the drawing room. I peeked out, to see a flare of black material, somebody's skirt, flutter out just as the person, whoever it was, disappeared around the corner of the upstairs corridor.

Mrs Bartleby. I was fairly certain it was her but thought I had better check. Quickly and quietly, I opened the door to the study, thinking I could say I had come to see if anyone wanted anything other in refreshments if I were challenged.

I could easily see who was in the room. Dorothy, who looked as though she was quite refreshed already, was dancing with Michael Harrison. Raymond Bentham was reclining on one of the armchairs by the window, with Arabella dancing attendance on him as usual. The gramophone was making so much noise, not to mention Dorothy shrieking with intoxicated laughter, that nobody noticed my quick entrance and equally swift exit.

I trailed downstairs and shut the kitchen door behind me. I was feeling somewhat nervous, given the telephone call, which I was now sure that Mrs Bartleby had listened to, and the inspector's words of warning to me. Why had Mrs Bartleby eavesdropped on our conversation? As I asked myself that question, it was with a wry recollection of my *own* eavesdropping of her conversation with Mrs Weston. Perhaps there was nothing sinister about it at all – perhaps, like me, she was just insatiably curious. *Or a snoop*. I swatted that little demon away once more.

Even so... As I began to prepare for afternoon tea (not that I imagined many people would be partaking after the festivities I'd just observed) and began to think about dinner, I was careful to keep an eye on both doors to the room. I remembered what had happened at Merisham Lodge. This time, there would be no Verity to save me if...if anything happened. She would have her hands full with Dorothy. For the first time in a while, it occurred to me that I was in the house with a murderer. Most probably. *Most definitely, Joan.*

I began chopping vegetables at the kitchen table, which at least meant I had the advantage of being able to see all about me. I thought back to my discovery of poor Mrs Ashford's body and tried to recollect exactly what had happened. Mrs Weston had said she'd found Mrs Bartleby in Mrs Ashford's room. Hadn't she? My rapid knife got slower as I thought back and tried to remember.

Just as I swept all my chopped vegetables into the pot on the stove, a shadow darkened the outside door and I jumped, despite all my precautions. Anxiety gave way to pleasure as I realised it was Inspector Marks.

"Good afternoon, Miss Hart."

"Please call me Joan," I said impulsively.

The inspector smiled. "Well, I will. Thank you." He hesitated a moment and said, almost shyly, "My Christian name is Tom."

I almost blushed. The thought of calling the inspector by his first name! I didn't say anything but nodded in confusion.

Inspector Marks – Tom – cleared his throat and sat down at the table. "What was it you wanted to tell me, Joan?"

I thrust aside all other considerations and became businesslike. "I overheard a strange conversation between Mrs Bartleby and Mrs Weston and it's made me...uneasy."

"Oh, yes?"

I sat down myself and folded my hands on the table. "I think – I think there may be another will. Another will of Mrs Ashford's."

The inspector had that look on his face that I

knew well, a kind of intensity, a concentration. It made me lean forward to look him directly in the face. "When Verity and I arrived, the first night we were here, Mrs Ashford asked us to sign something. A paper, a document. We couldn't see what it was we were signing but I have a feeling it was a will."

The inspector sat back, smiling. "You are a clever girl, Joan. It *was* a will. I've been speaking to Mr Brittain and Mrs Weston. Mrs Ashford wrote it out herself on the night of your arrival."

I nodded, pleased that I hadn't made a fool of myself. Then I frowned. "Sir, so, that was the will that Mr Brittain read out this morning?" I thought of Mrs Bartleby's anger and Mrs Weston's response. Something wasn't making sense. "But..." I stopped speaking, trying to work it out in my head.

The inspector leaned forward again. "I can't go into too much detail, Joan, as I'm sure you'll appreciate, but I can tell you that it wasn't the will that was read this morning. The one that Mr Brittain read out this morning was the legal will of Mrs Ashford. The...new will, I supposed you'd call it, *was* written, but it wasn't posted and in the event, it wasn't valid."

"Wasn't valid?"

"I won't go into technicalities with you, Joan, but the legal phrasing was wrong. This is quite common when people write out their own wills, I'm afraid. Makes a jolly mess when it comes to probate, apparently." He hesitated and added, "There was also a question – a suggestion, from Mrs Weston – that there may have been undue influence."

I raised my eyebrows. I could imagine who he meant. "I see," I said, slowly.

"Tell me what you overheard, Joan. In fact, tell me everything you can about Mrs Bartleby."

I did so, even though what I had to tell him wasn't much. He listened carefully and made notes in his little book. Even as I was speaking, and enjoying having the inspector listen to me so assiduously, there was a part of me that wanted to creep away and find a quiet space so I could just *think*. I had felt this before in previous situations, when I knew I could find the solution to the crime if I could just sit and think.

Just as I was drawing to a close, I heard footsteps in the corridor outside and glanced around. It was Verity, looking like thunder.

"Oh, I'm so sorry," she said, when she saw who was sitting at the table with me. "Good afternoon, Inspector Marks."

"Miss Hunter. What a pleasure." The inspector got up courteously. "Is there a problem?"

Verity glanced at me and in that short look, I knew exactly what the problem was and sighed inwardly. "Do you need me to come, V?"

She nodded, trying to smile unconcernedly.

"Please don't let me interrupt you, though. I can manage."

The inspector and I looked at one another. "You must help your friend, Joan." Verity's eyebrows twitched at the sound of my Christian name. "We can meet again soon." Verity's eyebrows were almost at her hairline. "I'll see myself out. Good day to you both, ladies."

He replaced his hat, tipped it to us and left by the back door. Verity allowed me thirty seconds of silence before she grabbed my arm. "*'Joan'? 'We'll meet again soon'?*"

I snorted. "It's nothing, V. He wanted to talk to me about the – the case, that's all."

"Hmm." The look she gave me told me that the subject was far from closed. To forestall her, I asked her what was wrong.

"Is it Dorothy?"

Verity rolled her eyes. "She's *incredibly* drunk. I'm not sure even you or I could get her up to bed between us."

"Oh, Lord." Thoughts of Inspector Marks flew out of my head. "I'll come and help."

Chapter Twenty

LAST THING THAT NIGHT, I sat down on my bed to unbuckle my shoes and rub my tired feet. *What a day*. Dorothy had indeed been so intoxicated that she could barely stand. When Verity and I had got back to the study, she'd been slumped on the chaise longue like a sack of potatoes. Arabella stared at her in alarm and Raymond, damn him, was openly laughing at her. I had to restrain myself from slapping his face as we walked past him.

Michael, fairly tipsy himself, sat next to her, patting her hand, saying, "Dotty, old girl? Wake up, what? Dotty?" Verity leant over and whispered something in his ear and he looked up, blinking in owlish confusion. Then, clearly understanding, he nodded.

Michael carried Dorothy up to her room. There were a few anxious moments on the stairs when he looked as though he might drop her – Verity and I stood poised to catch either of them – but disaster was averted. He plunked her down on her bed and she groaned and rolled over. I ran to get a bucket from the kitchen.

When I got back, Michael was gone, and I was too late with the bucket. Verity was sponging her mistress's face with a flannel. I sighed and helped her strip the counterpane and took it downstairs to soak. "Come and get me if you need anything," I whispered to her when I left and dropped a kiss on the top of her bright hair. She smiled at me gratefully.

Such had been the to-do that I hadn't really had a moment to think about what the inspector had told me. Now, in my room, I had the peace and quiet I needed. I undressed, washed, and cleaned my teeth and climbed into bed. I mustn't fall asleep before I had puzzled it all out... After a moment, I climbed back out and fetched my notebook and a pencil.

Now...the will. The will read this morning – was it only this morning? – had made beneficiaries of Arabella and Mrs Bartleby. Oh, and Michael, although a much smaller amount. I remembered Mrs Bartleby's gasp as it was read out. She had expected the *new* will to be read, of that I was now fairly certain. And she had been furious when the old will had been read instead. So that must mean that the new will had been much to her advantage, surely? Why on earth hadn't I asked the inspector what the new will had said, even if it hadn't been valid? Oh well, that was a question for when I next saw him. If Mrs Weston had suspected Mrs Bartleby of unduly influencing Mrs Ashford to change her will, that would explain why she hadn't posted the new will. I remembered how worried and lost she'd looked, which could now be explained. But why had Mrs Ashford changed her will?

I looked up from the notebook and remembered the row she'd had with Arabella. What had she said? Something about only one thing being able to change Arabella's mind? Was that what she had meant?

But, as far as I was aware, Arabella wasn't aware of the new will. But Mrs Bartleby had been. So what did that mean?

I looked down at my scribblings. What that meant was that Mrs Bartleby had had a big motive for Mrs Ashford's death. I remembered Mrs Weston saying she'd found her with Mrs Ashford in the bedroom *after Mrs Ashford had died*. With a chill, I also remembered something Inspector Marks had told me a long time ago. *Poison is a woman's weapon*. Had Mrs Bartleby attempted to poison Mrs Ashford, and when that hadn't succeeded, she'd finished her off with a blow to the head and attempted to make it look like an accident?

Both attempts had that in common, I realised. Both were supposed to look like accidents. Somebody wanted to get away with this murder.

I heard tired, dragging footsteps in the corridor outside and looked up sharply. I always locked my door last thing at night but I had made doubly certain it was bolted tonight. But then I realised it was just Verity. I heard the squeak of her bedroom door and, moments later, the creak of her bedsprings. Poor V. She'd obviously been up all evening with Dorothy. I felt a surge of anger at our mistress. How could she be so selfish and irresponsible?

I unbolted the door and crept next door. "It's me. Joan."

"Come in, Joanie." She sounded exhausted.

"I just wanted to make sure you were all right." I went in to Verity's room to find her flat on her back on her bed, still fully dressed. "Come on, V. You can't sleep in your clothes."

"At this moment, I don't care."

I helped her up and helped her undress. "How is Dorothy?"

Verity huffed. "She seems to be well enough to entertain young Michael in her room. That's why I could leave. He came back to 'see how she was'."

"Really?" Try as I might, I was a little scandalised. Even knowing Dorothy as I did, it seemed a little – well, *very* – fast.

"I tell you, Joanie, I really do not care anymore. I'm fed up with her." Verity pulled her nightdress down over her head with a cross yank. "If she calls for me later, I am *not* going."

I glanced at the clock. It was past midnight. "She surely wouldn't want you now?"

Verity chuckled wearily. "Not if she's doing what I think she's doing."

"V!"

"Oh, Joan. I need to go to bed."

"Yes, you do." I tucked her in and switched off the light. "Good night. We'll talk tomorrow."

"Night." I could hear her slipping into sleep even as she spoke.

My own eyelids were drooping. I went back to my room, bolted the door behind me and picked up my notebook. Probably best not to leave this lying around. I yawned and hid the notebook under my mattress. As I straightened up, my eyes fell on the suitcase on top of my wardrobe. Impulsively, I got up to fetch it down. Tired as I was, I wanted to look at my play, to remind myself of what I'd achieved. I needed to remind myself that I wasn't just a cook, I was more than a servant, that I had other talents.

Smiling, I popped the lock of the suitcase and raised the lid. Then the smile fell from my face at what I saw. The suitcase was empty. My play was gone.

WELL, THAT DIDN'T MAKE FOR a restful night's sleep, as I'm sure you can imagine. Tired as I was, I lay awake for what seemed like hours, staring up into the darkness and wondering what had happened. Had I moved the play and simply forgotten I'd done so? Surely not. Someone must have taken it, but who? And more importantly – why? What value could a play about a murder committed somewhere else and involving other people (all fictional but based on something that had happened to me) possibly have to someone else?

I eventually fell asleep from sheer exhaustion and woke up the next morning feeling like I'd been run over by an omnibus. Groaning, I pulled myself from my bed and began to prepare myself for the day ahead. My gaze kept returning to the suitcase, which I replaced on top of the wardrobe. For a paranoid moment, I was convinced that I'd dreamt the play disappearing and made myself check. The suitcase was still empty. I looked under the bed and in the dressing table. No sign of it. What an absolute mystery and something I found particularly distressing. Months of hard work had gone into that play, and I knew there was absolutely no hope of me being able to rewrite it exactly as it had been.

I stomped into the kitchen, feeling exceptionally fed up and cross. So preoccupied was I with the theft of my life's work, I'd almost forgotten the events of yesterday. When Verity asked me for a tray to take up to Dorothy, lifting up her eyes at the same time, I had a moment of wondering why she wasn't coming down to breakfast as normal.

"She probably won't get out of bed all day," Verity said, an edge of spite in her tone. Well, it was understandable. "I feel like spiking her tea with something horrid."

That made me smile. "I could suggest a few things."

Verity laughed. "No, don't tempt me, Joan." She took a closer look at me and frowned. "You look terribly pale."

I explained about my bad night. It was on the tip of my tongue to tell her about the mysterious disappearance of my play but I didn't. She didn't need anything else to worry her, and perhaps there was a simple explanation. But what?

I fortified myself with a pot of strong coffee and got on with the day's work. Thank goodness it was just to be a family dinner tonight, with only five to feed; that was if Dorothy managed to make it out of bed by then. I wondered, rather pruriently, whether Michael was still in her room. And the servants would want sustenance, of course. I wondered when Michael and Raymond would be able to go back to university. Perhaps after the inquest? And Mrs Bartleby... I thought about my ponderings of the previous night and wondered whether Inspector Marks would go so far as to arrest her. I hoped he would seek me out again, although I didn't feel as if I could justify telephoning him once more. Really, I had nothing more to tell him, except about the commonality of the murder attempts, both disguised as would-be accidents. Was that enough for me to contact him?

I was too tired to make a decision. The day dragged by. Mrs Weston made her first appearance downstairs for several days, coming into the kitchen just before dinner. She looked thinner and gaunter but the haunted look had gone from her face. Surprisingly, she thanked me quite warmly for making sure that everything had run smoothly in her absence.

Ethel and I carried the dishes up to the dining room. I was curious to see if Dorothy was there, and she was, though she was rather pale and shame-faced and drank only water. She didn't catch my eye. Indeed, she kept her gaze on her plate for the most part and spoke little. I wondered if perhaps this lapse into her previous bad habits had reminded her of how much she had to lose. Perhaps this was the real turning point?

It was only as I turned to go that I realised that Mrs Bartleby was nowhere to be seen. Michael seemed to come to the same conclusion a moment later.

"Why, where is Constance? It's not like her to be late for dinner."

Raymond looked bored and didn't answer. Arabella looked enquiringly over at the empty chair, as if she'd only just noticed. "I'm sure she'll be down in a minute," she said. She was sitting next to Raymond, of course.

"Well, we can't start without her," Michael said rather irritably. "Somebody had better go and rouse her." There was a moment's silence as nobody volunteered. Then Michael caught my eye. "Joan, do you think you could go and give her a knock? She's been in her room most of the afternoon. I suppose she's nodded off or something."

"Of course, sir." I bobbed a curtsey and made my way to the door.

Climbing the stairs to the first floor, I felt a qualm. Although I had no specific evidence that Mrs Bartleby was the killer, I had enough unease to make me hesitate before raising my hand to knock at her bedroom door. Don't be silly, I told myself. She's not going to hurt you. She doesn't know you know anything.

Silence followed my knock. I tried again. Still nothing.

"Madam?" I called softly as I tried the door handle. It wasn't locked. As I entered the bedroom, I had a flash of memory back to the day I went into Mrs Ashford's room to find her body. And as it turned out, this was exactly like that. Because when I opened the door and walked into Mrs Bartleby's room, I found her laid out on the bed, white and still. Dead.

Chapter Twenty-One

THE NEXT MORNING, THE HOUSE seemed full of policemen. They were thickest in Mrs Bartleby's room, naturally, but could also be found in the drawing room. There were even a couple in the kitchen, taking a statement from me whilst Ethel sat nearby, goggling silently.

"I was sent to call her down to dinner," I said. Inspector Marks sat once more at the table but this time, he and I weren't having a *tete a tete*. "She didn't answer the door so I knocked again and went into the room. I saw her straight away – she was lying on the bed." I took a deep breath and clasped my hands together under the table. Perhaps I wasn't quite as hardened to violent death as I thought.

"Go on, Miss Hart," said the inspector. We were back to formality again, although that could have been because of the others who were there. This wasn't the time to worry about it, anyway.

"I could see she was dead straight away." I repressed a shudder, remembering the horrible sight; the vomit, the foam on her lips. "I didn't touch her, not even to feel her pulse. I could see it was no good."

"Quite right," said Inspector Marks. "But I'd expect nothing less from you, Miss Hart."

We exchanged faint smiles and the sergeant sitting next to him and taking notes looked a little surprised. He gave me a glance that was slightly more respectful.

"I shut the door and went to tell Mrs Weston. It wasn't my place to call the police, but I knew she would have it in hand." I went on, telling them everything I could remember. When I got to the bit where the news had to be broken to the family and their guests, I tried to think back. Was there anybody in that room who hadn't looked quite as shocked as the others? But it was hopeless. I'd done my best, but even I couldn't watch four different faces at once. I'd watched Arabella and I could have sworn that the horror on her face was genuine.

Mrs Bartleby's death changed everything. Now I really *did* need time to sit and think. Fat chance of that happening now. And how was I going to get any meal prepared with all these policemen in my kitchen?

I was just about to speak up on that very point when the inspector forestalled me. "Mrs Bartleby left a note."

"A note?" I said, blankly.

CELINA GRACE

"Did you not see it? It was by her bedside table. A suicide note."

"*Suicide*?" I began blinking very fast. Mrs Bartleby had committed suicide? But what did that mean? Had I got everything wrong?

"That surprises you?" The inspector watched me closely.

"I must say it does, sir." I was suddenly filled with the urge to question Inspector Marks intently. But how? I cleared my throat. "Um... Inspector, I've told you all that I know. And I know the circumstances are...*special*, but there's still a house full of people who will need feeding. Do you think... Could your officers..."

Our eyes met, and I could see he understood exactly what I meant. I felt a surge of something – pleasure, perhaps, or anticipation. He understood me. What a rare and wonderful thing it is, to have someone truly understand you.

"Of course, Miss Hart. Gentlemen..." He stood up and began directing the officers towards the back door and the stairs. "There are plenty of rooms upstairs to use, and we must allow Miss Hart to get on with her work."

I spoke to Ethel. "Ethel, go up to your room and have a rest for ten minutes or so. I'll give you a call when I need you."

When Ethel had left and when the last blue uniform had filed out, Inspector Marks waited a moment and then turned to me. "Joan?"

184

THE HIDDEN HOUSE MURDERS

I fought the urge to grab his hands. "Do you *honestly* think it was suicide?"

He sat down at the table and gestured for me to do the same. "No. As it happens, I don't."

I leant forward. "How did she die?"

"The post mortem hasn't been performed yet, but I'd say it was a pretty clear case of cyanide poisoning."

Cyanide. Why did that ring a bell? I groped for the memory and eventually found it. Verity, telling me Arabella had said something to the police about cyanide being kept here to get rid of wasps. I told the inspector just that.

"I see. Thank you." He made a note in his little book. "So, Joan. I don't think it was suicide. In fact, I'd say it was murder. I *know* there's a murderer in this house. I need your help to find him. Or her. Can you help me eliminate somebody? Anybody?"

I nodded. "I'll do my best, sir."

"Please, Joan. You can call me Tom. If you like."

I blinked, astonished. "Oh. Oh, I – I don't know—"

Was the inspector blushing? "Well, I'll leave it up to you."

Now *I* blushed. I looked down at my lap, trying to recollect myself. *This is serious, Joan. Concentrate.* I looked up, straightening my shoulders. "Well, er – Tom—" I stumbled a little but hurried on. "I – um...

What I wanted to ask was when do you think Mrs Bartleby died?"

The inspector looked at his notes. "The doctor seems to think it was sometime in the early hours of last night. Perhaps one o'clock in the morning. Between one and three o'clock."

"Oh." I thought back. Really, at that hour, what hope did I have of knowing where anybody was, apart from in bed? *Bed*. That made me recollect something and I began to blush again, wondering whether I should say something.

"What is it?" The inspector could see that I had something to tell him.

Sorry, Dorothy. I sent the apology to her within my mind as I opened my mouth. "Well, er – Tom, I think Miss Drew and Mr Harrison can be eliminated because..." I trailed away. I was treading in dangerous waters.

"Go on, Joan."

I took a deep breath and told him what Verity had told me. "Of course, I know that doesn't necessarily mean much but – well – I thought I should tell you." My entire face felt like it was on fire.

"That's fine, Joan. I'll have to interview Miss Drew and Mr Harrison, of course, but it's useful to know." The inspector had become very matter-of-fact. "You can't tell me about anyone else?"

"I'm afraid not. I know Verity – Miss Hunter was fast asleep, but I couldn't say about anyone else." I thought back through my memories and recollections. There was something else I'd needed to tell the inspector about, wasn't there? After a moment, I recalled exactly what.

"Ins – er, Tom, there's one more thing I've thought of. The murder of Mrs Ashford – both attempts, I mean – they were designed to look like accidents. First food poisoning, or mushroom poisoning, and then, when that didn't work, the head injury disguised as a fall."

The inspector nodded, his eyes on my face (luckily, that had returned to its normal colour). "That's astute of you, Joan."

"So, it's very likely that this murder was disguised as something else as well." I thought of something else. "What did the note say? Mrs Bartleby's note, I mean?"

The inspector didn't say anything. Instead, he held out a piece of paper, using his handkerchief. "Don't touch it," he warned.

"Of course." I bent to read it. It was a piece of cream coloured notepaper, torn at the top and it was typed but had Mrs Bartleby's signature at the bottom. It was short. *I am sorry. I can't go on like this knowing what I know. I must do what's right for me.*

"Well," I said slowly. "That's not even very convincing, is it? It's clearly been torn off the end of a letter."

The inspector nodded. "I imagine it had to

suffice, at the last minute. The murderer thought it was worth a try."

I read those words again. *I can't go on like this knowing what I know.* "She was killed because she knew something, wasn't she?"

"Yes. She knew who killed Mrs Ashford."

"And the murderer thought she was going to tell. So he or she had to act quickly." I stopped speaking and the inspector and I stared at one another. "What's the motive?" I whispered, almost to myself. "If we knew the motive, we'd find the killer."

"Yes, that's true."

I leant forward again. "Who benefits from Mrs Ashford's death?"

Inspector Marks began to tick people off on his fingers. "Arabella. Mrs Bartleby. Michael Harrison. Mrs Weston."

I got up and paced around the kitchen. "Mrs Ashford was going to change her will. She got Verity and me to sign the new one."

"And that new will benefitted Mrs Bartleby."

I reached the far wall and turned on my heel to walk back. Walking helped me. "Arabella knew that her mother was going to change her will. I think she did, anyway. And Mrs Bartleby knew because she overheard. Mrs Weston knew because Mrs Ashford gave her the new will to post, although as it happened, she didn't. Michael – did he know?"

The inspector watched me closely. "I don't believe he did."

"He only inherits a small amount, anyway." I half laughed as I said it. What I wouldn't give for five thousand pounds of my own! "Is that the case with the new will?"

"Yes. The other bequests remained the same. The only change was that Arabella was, well, effectively disinherited."

I stopped walking and went back to my seat at the table. My mind felt so tangled up with confusion that for a moment, I found it difficult to speak.

After a moment, I looked at the clock. "Oh, help. Inspector – Tom, I mean – I really do need to get on with my work. I'm sorry."

"Of course you must." Inspector Marks became brisk and jumped to his feet. "Well, Joan, I must say how very helpful I've found our conversation."

I smiled at him. "Thank you. I hope I've helped."

"Very much so." He remained on his feet for a moment longer, looking at me as if he'd like to say more. Then he held out his hand. "Please take care of yourself, Joan. Telephone me if you think of anything else or if you feel in the slightest danger. I'm keeping a uniformed officer here."

That reassured me. "Thank you," I said once more.

"There will, of course, have to be an inquest. And inevitably, some press attention."

That hadn't occurred to me, but of course there

would be. I sighed inwardly, remembering the madness after the murders at Merisham Lodge.

Merisham Lodge. Something flickered in my memory, something so intangible I couldn't put my finger on what it was. Was it something to do with the house? With the people in the house? The more I tried to focus my attention on what it was, the more it eluded me before it slipped away altogether.

The inspector had obviously noticed my period of introspection. "What is it, Joan?"

"That's just it," I said in frustration. "I don't know. Something came back to me, from when we—" I stopped myself saying 'worked together' just in time. "When we were at Merisham Lodge. Something about that."

Inspector Marks waited patiently but after a moment, I shook my head, grimacing. "Sorry. It's just gone."

"Don't fret, Joan. If it's important enough, the thought comes back, I find."

I nodded. "Yes. I'm sure it will." My eyes went to the clock behind him on the wall. *Help.* I was so behind in what I had to do.

Astute man that he was, Inspector Marks noticed. He bid me goodbye, repeated that I was to contact him if I needed to, and then left.

Much as I wanted to sit down and puzzle over what I'd just half-remembered, I didn't have the time. I shouted up the stairs for Ethel and began to get to work.

Chapter Twenty-Two

THINGS HAD BEEN IN SUCH a state of kerfuffle that my missing play had quite slipped my mind. It wasn't until I was dressing myself the next morning that my gaze fell on my suitcase and I remembered. How could I have forgotten? I reached for the case and opened it, hoping against hope that the manuscript would be magically restored to its rightful place. Of course it wasn't. I put the suitcase back up on the top of the wardrobe. What on earth was going on? Why would anyone steal my play? Was it something to do with what was happening here?

I went downstairs through the silent house, nodding to the policemen who sat solidly by the front door. What a boring night he must have had. No doubt his replacement would be on the way and he could go off duty. I put the kettle on the hob and made him a cup of tea, which he accepted with pleased thanks.

As I prepared breakfast, I thought about my play. Was there the remotest possibility that the murderer could have removed it? The thought of a killer sneaking into my room didn't make me feel very comfortable. But why would they? But then, who else would have taken it? And why?

I was going around in mental circles. Ethel came into the kitchen a moment later, and I put her in charge of frying the bacon. As I began to plate up the trays to take to the dining room, I thought about what had happened. Again, that quicksilver flash of – *something* – something to do with Merisham Lodge. Oh, if only I had five minutes to myself to sit and *think*...

After breakfast, I managed to indicate to Verity that I needed to talk to her. She understood, of course, and carried her plate into the scullery.

"What's the matter?" she hissed.

I explained about my play. As she listened, I was astonished to see a guilty look cross her face.

"V? Do you know something about this?"

Verity bit her lip. "I didn't think you'd notice so quickly."

I was both utterly astounded and jolly annoyed. "What do you mean? *You* took my play?"

Verity began to giggle. "Yes, I did. Hear me out. Please, Joanie."

I stepped back a little, so my back hit the shelves behind me, and folded my arms. "I'm waiting."

"Well." Verity shook her red head airily. "I knew

you were never going to get around to doing anything with it. And I read it and, Joanie, it's awfully good."

Despite my anger, I was touched and then embarrassed. "No, it's not."

"Yes, it *is*, Joan. Anyway, you're such a scaredy-cat that I knew you'd never have the gumption to send it off to anyone—"

"Steady on," I protested, thinking this was rather harsh.

Verity eyed me cynically. "So, when were you going to send it off, eh, Joan?"

"Well—I—" I stuttered to a halt.

"Quite," said Verity. "So, I thought it was up to me to inform the rest of the world about your genius, *and* I happened to know that Tommy's director was looking for some new material, so, I crept in, pinched it and posted it off to him."

She gave me a big, pleased smile that I was too flabbergasted to return. "You sent my play off to a – a director?"

"Yes, Joan. And what's more, he likes it."

If I'd been stunned before, I was poleaxed now. "He likes it?" I gasped, feebly.

"He certainly does. In fact, he'd like to meet you the next time you're in London."

"When am I ever in London?"

"There are such things as trains, Joanie. And days off."

I was silenced once more. A director – a *theatre*

director – liked my play? Tommy, Verity's uncle, had been an actor for years and would no doubt know plenty of people connected with the theatre, so I had no reason to doubt that part of the confession. But, a director liked *my* play? Enough to meet me?

"Gosh," was all I said; a very inadequate way of describing my feelings.

Verity grinned. "I knew you'd be pleased."

Pleased wasn't quite the word I would have used to describe my feelings. As I cast around for something to say to explain them, Mrs Weston cleared her throat on the other side of the scullery door. "Joan? Verity? Time to be getting on with your work, I think."

We exchanged a guilty glance. "Talk to you later," Verity whispered, hurrying out. I tried to compose myself and took a deep breath, smoothing my apron before following her.

I had no time to sit and think about my play, or getting to London, or the murders. Mrs Weston and I had to go through the orders for the week, which always took up a good deal of time. But first, the dining room had to be cleared of the family's breakfast dishes. Ethel and I took our trays and walked up the stairs.

Not much had been eaten. I suppose it was understandable, given the circumstances, but I still had to suppress an exclamation of annoyance. That was an hour's hard work gone to waste, not to mention the actual waste of the food itself. Perhaps I could refashion the leftovers into something else; goodness knows I was used to doing that. Ethel and I loaded up the trays and turned to go, but as I did, one of the silver knives slipped from my tray to crash on the floor and then skidded under the chesterfield.

"Blast," I said.

"I can get it," offered Ethel.

"No, don't bother. Take that tray down and I'll be along in a minute." I set my own tray down on the floor and got down on my hands and knees behind the sofa to see if I could reach the knife.

It was difficult to reach it. For a minute, I scrabbled around blindly, trying with questing fingers to reach it but it was impossible. I was just about to get to my feet to go and get someone stronger than I to move the chesterfield when I heard the dining room door open and the sound of people – two, by the sounds of it – coming into the room. After a second, I realised it was Dorothy and Michael.

"Michael? You've been awfully quiet all morning. Is there something the matter?"

I froze in my hiding position. Should I get up immediately so they knew I was here? Suppose they thought I was eavesdropping?

The back of the chesterfield rocked a little as they sat down, mere inches from me.

"I don't know." Michael sounded troubled. "I'm not sure."

"Why, what do you mean?"

"Well, that's just it, old girl. I'm not sure – it's something I saw – oh, it's probably nothing."

I stopped worrying about eavesdropping and began to listen intently. Michael carried on talking. "Dashed difficult to know what to do. I mean, I wouldn't want to get anyone into trouble. But then, what if it's important? I mean, do I tell the police or not?"

Heart thumping, I listened ever more carefully.

Dorothy sounded worried. "The police? You've got something to tell them about this...all this awful mess?"

"Well, that's just it. Do I, or don't I?"

Just tell her what you saw, I screamed to him silently in my head. I was beginning to get cramp from being crouched on the floor but I forced myself to stay still. To reveal my position now would be a very bad idea, both with regard to the resulting embarrassment and because I really needed to hear what Michael knew.

Dorothy spoke low but urgently. "Michael, if you've got something to tell the police, you really must tell them." She hesitated and then said, "It might be very dangerous for you to keep whatever it is to yourself."

I couldn't have agreed more. She and I both

knew that murderers didn't stop at getting rid of possible witnesses if they could.

Perhaps the sincerity of her tone convinced Michael. "Dash it all, I believe you're right."

"So, what *did* you see?"

I held my breath. Michael took a deep one of his own. "Well, old girl, it's rum. That night poor old Aunt Margaret died – no, was it the night before? Anyway, the night we all got ill." He lowered his voice even further and I strained to hear him. "Well, I saw Arabella put something in her coffee. Aunt Margaret's coffee, I mean."

There was a moment's silence. Then Dorothy said sharply, "Where did you see this?"

Michael sounded unhappy. "In the hallway. There was a tray of drinks, coffee and whatnot, and I was just coming down the stairs when I saw Arabella drop something in a coffee cup and stir it."

"Well, she was probably just putting in some sugar."

"I don't know. It didn't look like sugar. It was powdery, not a lump of something." He was quiet a moment and then went on. "It's just... I didn't think anything of it, at first. I thought, I suppose, that it *was* sugar if I thought anything. But...it was the way that she looked when she turned around and saw me walking down the stairs. She looked shocked. Guilty, even." He stopped talking again for a moment. "Oh, damn it to hell. It's nothing, I'm sure. Can't be. I must have made a mistake."

Dorothy didn't answer him for a moment. Then she said, slowly and purposefully, "You probably did make a mistake. But you must still tell the police."

"Oh, hell. Do I really have to?"

"Yes." I heard and felt the sofa shift as Dorothy stood up. "Come on, we'll go and find that Inspector Marks right now and tell him."

"Hell," Michael said once more, but I heard him stand up too. Then I listened to their footsteps going towards the door and the squeak of the hinges as it opened and closed behind them.

At last I could move. Hauling myself to my feet with a groan, I dusted off my knees and thought about what I'd just heard. Collecting that errant knife could wait. I had other things to do.

Chapter Twenty-Three

I WAS FRANTIC TO TALK TO Inspector Marks myself but I couldn't. One, I had no idea where he was, and two, I had work to do. Michael's revelation about Arabella had started me thinking, but with no time to sit down and puzzle it out, I had to push it to the back of my mind and switch my train of thought onto professional tracks.

Once luncheon was served and eaten, I had a precious half hour in which to sit down with a cup of tea and take the weight off my feet for thirty minutes. I didn't. Instead, I left Ethel reading her film magazine at the table, absentmindedly munching on a teacake, and took myself off. I needed to see Verity, and I was pretty sure where I could find her.

Dorothy and Michael had driven off after luncheon, Andrew acting as chauffeur. I wondered if they were going to the police station or merely going somewhere *tete a tete*. Was Dorothy in love with him? Or was she, as she sometimes did, merely amusing herself? What did Michael think of Dorothy? I remembered he'd once been keen on Arabella. Odd, really, given how different she was to Dorothy, both in looks and in character. I sincerely hoped he wasn't after Dorothy for her money, but I supposed it was a possibility – she was very wealthy. Still, she was a big girl and able to look after herself. I dismissed the thought from my mind and knocked on the door of Dorothy's bedroom.

"Come in," said Verity's voice, and I smiled, pleased to have been right about her whereabouts. She looked surprised to see me. "Hullo, Joan."

"Hullo." I sat down on the edge of the bed. Verity was tidying Dorothy's dressing table; putting jewellery back in cases, returning make-up to the drawers and dusting the mirror.

"Have you got a bit of time off?"

"Yes, for a change. I needed to talk to you."

"Oh?" Verity stopped flicking the duster and turned to face me.

"Firstly, I never thanked you for – for sending off my play." I smiled at her. "It was a jolly nice thing to do. If a little presumptuous."

Verity laughed. "Well, you know me, Joanie. Presumption is my middle name."

"Ha! I thought it was something other than that."

"Such as?"

I grinned. "I'm not telling you."

She flicked me with the duster. "Oh, you. Anyway, you're welcome. I can't wait to see it performed. How exciting!"

"It might not get that far," I protested. "I haven't even met the director yet."

"But tell me you're going to?" Verity raised a threatening eyebrow.

"I am. I promise I am. In fact, if you have his address, I'll write to him tonight."

"Nothing simpler. I'll bring it to your room this evening." Verity sat down on the bed next to me. "Well, was that all you wanted?"

"No." I leant forward a little, dropping my voice. "I need to talk to you about... About the murders."

Verity sat back. "Oh, Joan. I don't know what I can tell you."

"I need to talk to *somebody*."

"What's wrong with the inspector?" Verity smiled slyly. "I'd have thought you'd have jumped at the chance for a cosy little chat with him."

I pinched her knee. "Enough of that."

"Come on, Joan. You *are* keen on him, aren't you?"

I wavered, torn between embarrassment and honesty. "Well..."

Verity took pity on me. "Well, never mind that. Sorry. Go on and tell me whatever it is you want."

I leant back against the foot-post of Dorothy's bed and told Verity everything I'd overheard. Then

I told her about the will and the confusion over the second will.

Verity listened silently but kept tidying. The frown on her face grew deeper and deeper as I went on.

"So, what do you think?" I asked, when I'd reached the end of my recounting.

Verity was silent for a moment. She hung the last of Dorothy's silk scarves on the hanger, smoothed it down and put it away in the wardrobe, remaining silent all the while.

"Well?" I prompted.

Verity turned around to face me. Biting her lip, she came over and sat next to me once more on the bed. "There's something I haven't told you," she said.

My heart began to thump. "What?"

"Oh, it's nothing like *that*. I wasn't trying to keep anything from you, Joan, I just didn't even think of it until now." She sighed and said, "I heard from Dorothy, the night – you know, the night that everyone got ill..."

She paused. "Yes?" I said, trying not to let my impatience show.

"Dorothy said that Arabella was in an awful state that night. She'd had a row with her mother – I mean, Mrs Ashford – that one you overheard, Joan, but it was more than that." I leant forward, eager to hear more. "Apparently, you know she was keen as mustard on that Raymond?"

202

"That was obvious," I said, with a roll of my eyes. "*Is* obvious."

"Well, yes. Well, apparently, according to Dorothy, Arabella found out that day that Raymond had a lady friend, up in Cambridge."

"Oh." For a second I was nonplussed. "Well, he and Arabella weren't engaged or anything? Were they?"

"Oh no, nothing like that. To be fair, he hadn't done anything wrong. But I think it was a big shock to Arabella. Perhaps she'd convinced herself that he was keen on her and then, once she found out about his Cambridge sweetheart, realised that he wasn't."

"Hmm." Whilst it was good to hear this, I wasn't sure it had much bearing on what had happened. Or did it? I decided I would tell Inspector Marks and let him be the one to decide. "Was there anything else?"

Verity shook her head, red curls bouncing. "I can press Dorothy for more, if you like. Once she's come back."

"Has she gone to the police station?"

Verity nodded. "Goodness knows what time they'll be back."

"I suppose I had better assume that both she and Michael will be back for dinner." I caught sight of the clock on the mantelpiece and groaned. Half an hour didn't last long, these days. "No rest for the wicked. I'd better go."

"I'll let you know what happens with Dorothy later on."

"Thank you, V." I squeezed her arm as I hauled myself off the bed. I was tempted to just let myself fall backwards into the pillowy softness of the counterpane and go to sleep. But there were dishes to prepare and a murderer's motive to figure out... Again, I had that funny feeling, something to do with Merisham and Asharton. I couldn't help but think that my intuition was trying to tell me something, but what?

I waved to Verity as I trudged from the room, wondering if I could work it out by myself. At least the mystery of my missing play was cleared up. As I walked back down to my basement abode, I let my thoughts run ahead of me. How wonderful would it be to see a play of mine, an actual, real play of mine, performed on stage?

It will probably never happen, I told myself, but despite that, I couldn't help a little surge of excitement at the possibility. Oh, to be able to see into the future! And to see into the past as well. Then I could see for myself who had killed two people already.

The smile fell from my face. *Keep your wits about you, Joan.* I marched into the kitchen. Reaching for my apron, I went to rouse Ethel from her contemplation of those glossy black and white images of the stars of the silver screen. "Come on, Ethel. Time to get back to work."

Chapter Twenty-Four

I WAS JUST PUTTING THE PORRIDGE pot into the scullery sink to soak the next morning when there was a thunder of feet on the stairs from the hallway and a moment later, Verity almost fell into the kitchen. Ethel and I looked up in surprise.

"Joan, come quickly. Now!"

"What is it?" I asked, frightened. Beside me, Ethel put a hand to her mouth and gave a little squeak.

"It's Arabella. She's been arrested."

"What?" I dropped the tea-towel I was holding on the floor. "*Arrested*?"

"Come now. Inspector Marks is taking her away."

I didn't need telling twice. Verity and I dashed for the stairs, leaving poor Ethel behind us, no doubt in a state of utter confusion. We pounded up the stairs into the hallway and then Verity stuck a hand out to stop me, so quickly that I almost skidded over on the polished boards of the hallway. A moment later, I saw why. Mrs Weston was standing in the open doorway, looking outside to where Arabella was being supported down the front steps by two uniformed officers. Or so it first appeared. As I took another look, I realised she was being restrained, not supported. Each burly officer had a hand on her upper arm, one each side.

Dorothy, Michael and Raymond stood by the doorway to the dining room. Michael and Dorothy were holding hands and looking upset. My eyes flashed to Raymond's handsome face. He looked... *amused*? Surely not. As if he'd heard my thoughts, his gaze turned to mine and the expression on his face changed to something more serious.

Wondering if I'd imagined that fleeting look of...of glee, it had seemed, I turned my attention to Mrs Weston. With a shock, I realised she was crying. Her face was impassive, just as neutral as a good servant's should always be, but tears welled up and overflowed down her expressionless face.

Beside me, Verity rummaged in a pocket and pulled out a handkerchief. She shook it out, moving towards Mrs Weston and gently touching her on the arm, offering it.

"Oh, Verity. Thank you." Mrs Weston's face may have been impassive but her voice was not. It shook. "Please, girls, return to your work. There's nothing to be done here."

"Can I..." I began, without really knowing what it was I wanted to say.

Dorothy stepped forward. "Come and sit down for a moment, Mrs Weston. We've all had a terrible shock. Do come and sit for a moment and have a drink of something. For the shock."

Verity tensed beside me. I knew exactly what she was thinking. Hastily, I said "I'll make and bring up some tea, Madam."

"Thank you, Joan." Dorothy sounded distracted. She and Michael stepped back to allow Mrs Weston to walk into the drawing room in front of them. They all filed in, and Raymond shut the door behind himself.

Verity and I exchanged appalled glances, left alone in the hallway. "My God, if she starts again—" Verity began.

"Shush!" I dragged Verity towards the kitchen stairs, terrified of being overheard. We clattered back down to where Ethel was still waiting for us in the kitchen, her eyes like saucers.

"What's happening?" she squeaked.

"Don't fret yourself into a tizzy," I said, patting her on the arm. "We'll be all right."

"But what... Is it Miss Arabella?"

"The police just wanted to ask her some questions," I soothed. "It'll be fine, Ethel, don't worry."

"But—"

"Just get on with your work, there's a good girl, eh?"

Still squeaking a little, like a distressed mouse,

Ethel allowed herself to be shepherded back to the scullery. I shut the door on her and came back out, catching Verity's eye and jerking my head towards the back door.

We hurried to the same spot where I'd sat with Inspector Marks – Tom – the other day. It was a grey, still sort of day, white-skied but warm. The leaves on the trees were almost fully out now, and a lush green canopy spread over our heads.

"So, what happened?" I clutched at Verity's arm.

Verity blew out her cheeks. "Oof, Joanie, I don't know the ins and outs of it. All I know is that Dorothy came back from seeing the inspector and told me that she'd told him all she knew – what Michael saw and the state Arabella was in on the night everyone got sick. Then she came home. That's all I know."

I sat back, releasing her arm. "Tom – I mean the inspector – must have thought those were sufficient grounds to arrest her."

Verity was watching me. "Well, Joan, she's got the biggest motive, hasn't she? She was about to be disinherited."

"Was she, though? Did she know that?" I thought of what I was saying and shook my head. "How stupid of me, of course she knew that. I heard Mrs Ashford, well, *threaten* her with it." I thought for a moment. "And Arabella knew where the cyanide was kept. She said so." I paused again. There was something about that that troubled me. I voiced it aloud. "But, if you wanted to kill someone with cyanide and get away with it, why would you draw attention to the fact that you know where that particular poison is kept?"

"That's easy," Verity said cynically. "She was shamming. What do they call it, a double bluff?"

"Maybe." I wasn't convinced. But then I didn't really know where I was with this situation, did I? I felt hopeless for a moment, as if I were trapped in a cage, simply pacing around and around in circles, the illusion of movement disguising the fact that I wasn't going anywhere.

Verity took my hand. "Joan, I don't want to speak out of turn but I can see that this is eating you up. You're fretting terribly about finding out who did this and you mustn't." She paused and spoke very deliberately. "*It's not your job to find out.*"

We stared at each other for a moment. Then I sagged. "Perhaps you're right."

"I know you want to help, but there comes a time when you just have to accept that it's out of your control." She paused and said, diffidently, "Besides, I need you right now. I can just see what's going to happen."

I looked at her. "Dorothy, you mean?"

Verity nodded unhappily. "I can recognise the signs."

I thought for a moment and then pushed thoughts of the murders from my mind. It took quite a mental effort. "All right. What can I do to help?"

"Help me get her away from the cocktail cabinet, if she hasn't started all ready. If I can just distract her..."

"By doing what?"

Verity chewed her lip. "I might suggest she go shopping. Or maybe to the talkies. Yes, that's it. I'll see if I can get her to go out for a bit—"

Still talking, she gestured for me to follow her and we walked back to the kitchen. Ethel was measuring out flour at the kitchen table, and I gave her a reassuring smile as we walked past. "I'll be just a minute, Ethel. Carry on with what you're doing."

Mrs Weston was just emerging from the drawing room as we reached the hallway. Believing herself to be unobserved for a moment, her face crumpled. Then, as she heard our footsteps and saw us, she straightened up, becoming neutral once more. "Oh, girls, where is that tea?"

I cursed inwardly; I'd totally forgotten to make it. "It's on its way, Mrs Weston," I said, hastily, trying to beam a silent message to Ethel down below our feet.

"Miss Drew is asking for you, Verity," said Mrs Weston. She raised the twisted handkerchief to her eyes for a second. "I'm sure I don't know whether I'm coming or going today, I truly don't. There's poor Mrs Bartleby's room to be seen to and goodness

THE HIDDEN HOUSE MURDERS

knows how many for dinner. Surely, this situation with Miss Arabella is some mistake?"

She sounded desperate. I restrained myself from patting her arm and merely said, in as soothing a tone as possible, "Don't you worry about dinner, Mrs Weston. I'll make enough for...for everyone."

"Oh, thank you, Joan. Miss Drew is calling Mr Brittain right this moment—" She broke off, clearly wondering why she was telling me this piece of information. I smiled to put her at her ease.

It seemed incredible but in the turmoil and drama, I'd almost forgotten Mrs Bartleby. She'd been murdered because – why? Because she knew something, something about Mrs Ashford's murder. Was it possible that *she* had killed Mrs Ashford? Because she thought she would inherit the majority of the estate because Mrs Ashford had altered her will? But if that were the case, why had she died? Had she truly committed suicide out of remorse for what she'd done?

All these questions were buzzing around in my head, so much so that I barely noticed that Verity had gone into the drawing room. I tiptoed to the open door and inclined my head towards the gap to listen. From what I heard, it seemed unlikely that Verity was going to persuade Dorothy to go to the pictures. I could hear Dorothy speaking on the telephone, in a voice very unlike her usual, drawling, languid tone.

"Yes, Mr Brittain, arrested. I know. Yes, I know.

It's imperative that you attend the police station, as soon as you can. Miss Ashford needs you. Yes, I do understand—"

Footsteps came towards the door and I straightened up hurriedly and quickly walked away. I didn't see who emerged but after a moment, Verity's voice made me look behind me. She hurried towards me, looking relieved.

"Is she all right?" I asked, meaning Dorothy.

Verity nodded, widening her eyes to indicate her relief. "For the moment. She's trying to organise legal representation for Arabella."

I didn't let on that I knew. "Well, that's something, at least."

Verity followed me down into the kitchen. Ethel, that obedient child, was deep into the breadmaking. Hurriedly, I filled the kettle and slung it onto the gas.

"I'd better take that up," Verity said once I'd made it.

"Yes, you better had." I hesitated for a moment, wanting to talk to her about what had happened but realising with reluctance that this was neither the time nor the place.

She tipped me a wink and hefted the tray. "I'll see you later, Joanie. Don't think too much."

I snorted and waved her away. Then I turned back to the table and began to help Ethel. Perhaps Verity was right. There was a houseful of distressed people to feed and I needed to concentrate on that.

Chapter Twenty-Five

ARABELLA DID NOT RETURN FOR dinner. I don't suppose any of us really believed that she would. Her place, along with Mrs Ashford's and Mrs Bartleby's seats, sat horribly empty. Still, she was alive and in no danger, safely incarcerated in the local police station. Ethel and I carried the dinner dishes into the dining room, where the others were sat around the table in silence. Only three now. Michael and Dorothy looked unhappy, Raymond looked, as usual, rather bored. I was glad to leave and return to the kitchen.

Mrs Weston didn't join the rest of the servants for dinner, either. I carried a tray to her room and she took it from me at the door with a murmured, "Thank you, Joan," but that was all. Her eyes were red-rimmed, and it was obvious she had been crying. It would have been impertinent, not to mention cruel, to have commented. Ethel, Verity and I ate our own meal in subdued silence. It was Andrew's evening off.

Even as I ate, I was thinking furiously. Was Arabella guilty? I reviewed the evidence against her as I scraped the last of the mashed potato from my plate. The motive – she was about to be disinherited. That was inescapable. Michael's testimony of seeing her put something in her mother's – adoptive mother's – coffee. Could he have lied? Why would he? He had sounded completely convincing, and one thing I was good enough at, by now, was ascertaining whether someone was telling a falsehood or not. Of course, it was harder when you couldn't see their face as they were speaking, but I was fairly convinced he was telling the truth. But could he have been genuinely mistaken? It could have been that Arabella really was stirring sugar into Mrs Ashford's coffee. Or perhaps a medicine, or a tonic, or something like that. I made a mental note to ask Inspector Marks whether they had spoken to Doctor Goodfried on that subject.

But, on the debit side, I knew arsenic was bitter. Coffee would have disguised the taste and, as I knew Arabella was normally responsible for pouring out the coffee, she could have added a little to each cup, enough to make everyone suitably ill. Then a bigger dose for Mrs Ashford, intended to be fatal. I shivered inwardly.

But the poison hadn't worked. Or it hadn't worked quickly enough for the murderer's liking. As a frail, old woman, Mrs Ashford may have eventually died from her illness, but perhaps that would have been too uncertain an outcome for the murderer to risk. One thing I was convinced about was that the matter of the will – or wills – was of prime importance. Arabella couldn't risk Mrs Ashford changing her will. So, when the poison wasn't sufficient, a more drastic measure had to be introduced. A quick blow to the head of an elderly woman too weak to resist and then pose the body as if she had fallen and hit her head. No suspicion of foul play. The sickness of everyone was to be attributed to the consumption of wild mushrooms. The fall and resulting death of an old, sick lady merely an unfortunate accident. Was that how it had been?

"Joan. Wake up. You're miles away."

I started. Verity gently nudged me with her foot under the table. "Oh, sorry."

"You're wool-gathering. Didn't I tell you to stop thinking?"

I smiled reluctantly. "Well, you know me."

"Yes, I do. Come on, I'll help you and Ethel with the washing up. Then we can go to bed early."

Ethel and I were both cheered by this suggestion. Between the three of us, we quickly cleared the kitchen and prepared it for the next day.

I had been looking forward to a chat with Verity before retiring, but Dorothy had other plans. She and Michael were apparently heading out to the pictures, and she needed Verity to help her change.

Rolling her eyes and muttering, Verity stomped upstairs. I dismissed Ethel and stood for a moment in my peaceful, silent kitchen, thinking, for once, that I didn't have such a bad job. Then I made myself a cup of cocoa and carried it up to my room.

I undressed, slipped on my night dress, and bolted my bedroom door. Then, retrieving my little notebook from its hiding place, I climbed into my creaking bed. I was going to note down all the thoughts I'd had over dinner to see if they made more sense when set down in black and white.

My cocoa had almost gone cold by the time I'd finished writing. Hurriedly, I threw its cooling dregs down my throat and re-read what I'd written. Would it reveal anything I'd not seen before?

I read through once and then once more. I was conscious of some sort of creeping unease. Something about my conclusions was wrong, but what? What had I missed?

I sat back, feeling the hard poles of the bedstead against my back, and stared ahead. I thought back to the night when everyone had become ill. How long ago that now seemed, although it could have only been little more than two weeks. Mrs Weston had been attending Mrs Ashford – was that right? And Mrs Bartleby had been in that room. Dorothy had been with Arabella. Then Mrs Weston had gone into Arabella's room... Had Arabella ever been on her own? Had she been on her own long enough to creep into Mrs Ashford's room to finish what she'd started?

I stared down at my scribbled notes, feeling a coldness at the back of my neck. If my memories were correct, I didn't think she had. I didn't see how she could have done it.

After a moment, I glanced at my little clock. It was close to eleven o'clock at night. Far too late to ordinarily make a telephone call, but these were special circumstances, weren't they? Did I dare? After hesitating for almost a minute, I pushed back the covers and swung my legs out of bed. At least, at this hour, I was fairly certain of where I could find Inspector Marks.

I felt a qualm of fear as I unbolted my door. After a moment's thought, I went back and retrieved my hot water bottle from beneath my bed. It had been too warm to worry about filling it up for several days now, but it would do as an excuse for wandering the house after dark if I happened to be challenged. I knew that there was no policeman standing guard tonight – the station couldn't spare a man, given how hard they were now working on this baffling case.

The house seemed very big and very empty. I could hear faint sounds as I crept down the stairs past the family's bedroom floor; the murmur of voices on the wireless, the creak of a floorboard, the slam of a wardrobe door. I held my breath and hurried faster down to the hallway and tiptoed over the black and white tiles to the kitchen stairs at the back. The grandfather clock that stood in the corner of the hallway tick-tocked dolefully as I went past, and its minute hand jerked ever onwards. I was beginning to feel nervous; not so much about whether I could be in danger or not, but whether I really was calling the inspector far too late. He was probably fast asleep. Oh well, I would try and get through to him, and if not, would leave a message for him to call me on the morrow.

I could hear raucous, rather drunken laughter and song when the telephone was finally answered at the inn. I had some difficulty making the landlady understand who it was I needed to talk to but after a lengthy pause, so lengthy as to make me wonder whether I should just give up and put the receiver down, Inspector Marks' voice could be heard on the other end of the line.

"Joan," he exclaimed, I hoped in pleasure rather than annoyance. "It's late. Is everything all right?"

"Quite all right, sir, I mean...Tom." I was glad he couldn't see the colour of my face. It still seemed dreadfully forward to be able to call him by his first name. "It was just...I wanted to talk to you about Arabella Ashford."

There was a moment of his silence that was audible even over the hubbub of the bar behind him. He cursed and then apologised. "Sorry, Joan.

It's just – I wish we could have this conversation somewhere quieter."

It was my turn to apologise. "I'm sorry."

"Don't be. What was it that you wanted to tell me?"

I took a deep breath. "Sir – Tom – I don't believe Arabella could have done it. I know she's got the best motive and so forth, but from what I recall, and I'm fairly sure my memory is correct, she was never left alone on the night her mother died. Somebody was always with her."

Silence (against a background refrain of drunken laughter and the musical tinkle of a broken glass) from Inspector Marks. I wasn't sure if he was waiting for me to say more or if he was merely taken aback at my conclusions. I pressed on. "So I don't see how she could have struck the killing blow. To have done that, moved the body and got back into her room without anyone seeing her. I just don't see how she could have done it."

There was another pause and then the inspector spoke. He sounded apologetic, as if he didn't really want to have to say what he was going to say. "Joan, she confessed."

For a moment, I thought I'd misheard him. "*What*?"

"Arabella confessed. She confessed to the murder of her mother."

Aghast, I took the receiver from my face and

stared at the mouthpiece, as if it were playing tricks on me. Faintly, I could hear Inspector Marks asking "Joan? Joan, are you there?" but for a moment, it was all I could do to listen.

Chapter Twenty-Six

ARABELLA HAS CONFESSED. THAT WAS the sentence that went around and around my head, both through the night and all the next morning. I'd lain awake for long hours, looking up at the dim outline of the ceiling light through the darkness, thinking of how wrong I'd been. I'd been so sure that it hadn't been her. After a fitful sleep of a few hours, I'd dragged myself from my bed and threw some water at my face. I felt bone-tired. My feet dragged wearily down the stairs as I followed Ethel to the kitchen. *Arabella has confessed.* I'd been wrong then, so wrong.

As the morning's work got underway, I found myself beginning to sink into those all too familiar feelings of humiliation and shame. Who was I, to think of myself as a great detective? What did I actually think I was doing? It was only due to Inspector Marks' great kindness and forbearance that he hadn't torn a strip off me for having the temerity to try and tell him his job. He'd arrested

Arabella because of the compelling evidence against her and here was I, trying to tell him that he was wrong. It would serve me right if he never spoke to me again.

Luckily, it was bread-making day that day, and I took my frustrations out on the dough, lifting and pounding it as if it had done me an injury. Ethel looked quite alarmed at the vicious pummelling I gave the poor, inanimate lump. I wiped sweat from my brow and carried on. It was making me feel a tiny bit better.

As I slid the shaped loaves into the oven, I tried to forget the rest of the conversation I'd had with the inspector last night. But it was impossible. Arabella had confessed to the murder of her adoptive mother.

"Of course, she said she didn't actually mean to kill her." Inspector Marks hadn't sounded reproachful; quite cheerful, if anything. "She told me she just wanted to make her a little ill for a while, to give Arabella time to persuade Mrs Ashford to change her mind about the will. But she was frightened that she might get into trouble for that – of course – so she decided that if everyone else came down with mushroom poisoning, or what looked like mushroom poisoning, it would be much safer for her."

I'd been so flabbergasted, I'd barely been able to speak. "But..." I began. Then I took a deep breath. "What about the... What about the head injury?"

Now Inspector Marks had sounded more serious. "Arabella swears blindly that she didn't hit her mother."

"But—" I said again.

"Joan, we have to examine the possibility that Mrs Ashford really did have a fall. The evidence for the head injury was inconclusive."

"But, the drag mark—"

The inspector's voice softened. "Joan, you did well to spot that but it is a very small piece of evidence. It could be purely circumstantial. It's not enough to convict a person."

I was feeling so topsy turvy I barely recalled the only other question I had to ask him. After a moment of mental flailing, it came back to me. "But...Mrs Bartleby—"

Now Inspector Marks' voice hardened. "She's still being questioned about that. I'm not happy with her answers. She says she didn't do it, but—" He had paused and then said, more softly, "Joan, get some sleep. There's nothing more you can do tonight and you can leave it with me."

RECALLING MYSELF TO THE PRESENT, I felt my cheeks burn again at that remark. Was he warning me off? Had I truly overstepped the mark? I realised I was standing stock-still in the middle of the kitchen, staring blankly in to the distance and ignoring Ethel, who was asking me about the dinner plans for the day. "What's that?"

"Sorry, Joan. I was just wondering what we have to do for dinner. Only, it's my afternoon off, and I didn't know if you needed extra help—"

I shook myself mentally and tried to focus. "Oh, Ethel, don't worry. I'm sure I'll be fine. Let me take a look at the menu and we'll see."

I fetched my book and opened it to the right page, running a finger down the writing there. "Hmm. Chicken and potato pie. Well, that should be simple enough. There should be a chicken in the ice-box, could you fetch it for me?"

As Ethel rummaged around in the chilly depths of the ice-box, I couldn't stop myself thinking once more about last night. Again, I felt that flash of something – that fine needle of clarity, obscured by the thinnest layer of doubt in my mind. What had Merisham Lodge taught me that I couldn't remember?

Ethel returned with the bird, trussed up in brown paper and string. I unwrapped it, checking whether it was still good to eat.

"It's a bit small," said Ethel, dubiously.

"Perhaps," I said. "But there's only three to dine and us lot. We'll have to manage. I'll bulk it out with potatoes."

"You really need two of them," said Ethel.

Inspiration shot up like a firework, in a shower

of sparks. I shrieked, making Ethel jump. I turned to her and grabbed her up in a hug, making her jump even more. "Two of them! Ethel, you wonderful creature!" I squeezed her tight and then let her go.

Released from my arms, Ethel backed away slowly, as if in the presence of someone quite mad. "Mrs – Joan?"

I started laughing, partly from relief, partly from the look on her face. "Oh, Ethel, I'm sorry. Don't you mind me."

"Have I done something wrong?"

"*No*. No, please don't worry. Look, you go and get changed and enjoy your afternoon out. Don't worry about a thing."

As Ethel left the room in a hurry, still casting me nervous glances over her shoulder, I sat down at the table and stared at the chicken's goose-pimpled skin. *Of course*. How could I have been so stupid, so blind? That's what Merisham Lodge had taught me. I'd known it all the time but somehow, the penny had never quite dropped. *Of course*. Perhaps I was cleverer than I thought.

Moving as if my life depended on it, I wrapped up the chicken again, stowed it back in the ice-box and stood, poised for action. *Think, Joan*. After a moment, I realised I needed Verity. Yes, I most definitely needed her. She had skills that I didn't, even if I now knew I was on the right track. It explained everything but I needed *proof*. I needed evidence before I could go back to Inspector Marks. Where was Verity?

I stood for a second, almost vibrating with energy, unsure of where to go first. Then, recalling I had just touched raw chicken, I quickly washed my hands, dried them, patted my hair back into place and set off for the stairs. I knew what I had to do but I couldn't do it without Verity. I needed her and I needed her *now*, Dorothy or no Dorothy.

Chapter Twenty-Seven

AS LUCK WOULD HAVE IT, I found her easily. She was cleaning Dorothy's jewellery, sitting quietly at the dressing table in Dorothy's room with her head bent down over the sparkling jewels. I observed her for a moment without her seeing me and felt a surge of affection. Dearest V. No matter what happened in our lives, I knew that I would always have her there, in spirit if not in person. It was at that moment that I realised that neither of us were orphans. Not anymore. We had each other.

She looked up then and saw me and smiled. "Hullo, Joanie. Got a few minutes to yourself for a change?"

"Not really." I came into the room, ruminations on our friendship forgotten. I remembered what it was I wanted her to do. "Actually, I need your help."

Verity looked alert. "Oh?"

I sat down on the bed and clasped my hands together. "I need you to search a room."

Verity's finely marked eyebrows shot up. "*Oh?*" she said again, with added emphasis.

"Mrs Bartleby's room."

A fine silver chain slithered from Verity's fingers. "Now, Joan, what are you up to? What's going on?"

I fixed her with my gaze. "I think I know who the killer is."

Verity flinched. "Shush, Joan! Keep your voice down."

She was right. "Sorry." I leant forward and whispered. "I know what happened. The murders, I mean."

Verity leant forward too, so that we were almost nose to nose. "Well, gosh, Joan. Are you going to tell me?"

"Of course. But while I do, I need you to search Mrs Bartleby's room."

Verity gave me a look. "You do know the police have done that already?"

I grinned at her. "But they aren't housemaids and they don't know all the hiding places."

Verity laughed out loud. "True! Well, if you think it'll help…"

"It will help. I know what happened—" I was forced into honesty. "Well, most of it. I think. But I need proof. Inspector Marks has already had a confession out of Arabella."

That stopped Verity in her tracks as she walked to the door. "Blimey. Really?"

"Yes." I hastened, conscious of time ticking

away. "Come on. Let's do it quickly. You can borrow my spare pair of gloves."

VERITY CLOSED DOROTHY'S BEDROOM DOOR behind her and we hurried to Mrs Bartleby's room. Once more, I was struck with the advantage, strange as it might seem, that we had by being servants. No one would question why we were in a certain place, providing we looked as though we were working. Verity had been a housemaid for years before she became a lady's maid. What she didn't know about secret hiding places wasn't worth knowing.

Once we were in the room, I grabbed up a stack of linen from the wardrobe, just to add credence to my being there. Of course, any *servant* would have asked why the cook was doing the housekeeping, but I didn't think it would occur to any of the gentry.

Verity began to search the room while I stood guard at the door. It was a very feminine room, rather overblown in decoration, with heavy emphasis on floral patterns. Nothing like as stylish as Dorothy's room was back in London.

As I watched Verity get on her hands and knees to feel about under the bed, I began to feel something very like a niggle of anxiety. Quite apart from being here in this room, I was beginning to be aware of a rising uneasiness. If I was right in my theory (and I thought I was), then why had Arabella confessed? Why *now*, after Constance Bartleby was already dead? That part didn't make sense at all.

Verity was almost nose to nose with the floorboards now. I knew that the police would have thought of searching under and even within the mattress, but then the police didn't know that most bedrooms had an easily lifted piece of floorboard. That was what Verity was looking for now – I knew it without asking her.

"Help me get this rug up, Joan," she asked, beginning to roll the heavy Persian rug back from the floor. I bent to assist her.

Once we moved it, Verity resumed her close search and gave a cry of triumph. "There we are, Joan! What did I tell you?" Actually, she hadn't told me anything but it didn't matter. I got her meaning. She got up and retrieved a nail file from a pot on the dressing table, knelt down again and inserted the file. Slowly, she levered up the piece of floorboard until it came free entirely.

Breathless with anticipation, I joined her in kneeling on the floor and peered into the space under the floorboards. It was empty.

"Oh," I said, disappointment evident in my tone.

Verity gave me a wink. "Don't worry, Joan. This is only the *first* hiding place. Even if the police had found this – which I don't believe they did– they wouldn't have known where to look for the actual hiding place." While she was speaking, she leant down and groped with her arm in the dusty space beneath the floorboard. "Should be – just about – ah!" A second later, she withdrew her arm with a small wooden box clasped in her gloved hand.

I clasped my own hands together in excitement, heedless of the fact that my one spare pair of white gloves were now the colour of dust. "Verity, you are a miracle worker."

"It might be nothing," Verity warned. "But, well, let's just say I've been asked to hide some, erm, *interesting* things in this kind of hidey hole."

I nearly asked, "For Dorothy?" but decided against it. Besides, in Dorothy's case, I could imagine the kind of things that were hidden, poor woman. Bottles and hip flasks, probably.

I let Verity open the box because she was the only one wearing gloves. It was a small, nondescript box and, when the lid was opened, it seemed to contain only one object, a folded piece of paper. Disappointment struck me anew. The paper wasn't even thick enough to be a folded letter. Verity lifted it carefully and opened it up.

As she read it, a gleam of light glinting from something else in the box caught my eye. I peered closer. I had just realised that it was a gold ring when Verity gasped.

"What is it?" I asked, heart leaping up into my throat.

She said nothing but held the unfolded paper in

front of my eyes so I could see for myself. I saw what was written on it and realised that I had been quite wrong – about almost everything. I gulped.

Verity's wide eyes met mine. "This changes everything," she said quietly.

"Yes. It does."

There was much we had to do but for a moment, all we could do was sit there by the dark little hole in the floorboards, staring at the wavering sheet of paper in Verity's faintly shaking fingers.

Chapter Twenty-Eight

"THANK YOU ALL FOR JOINING me here this evening," Inspector Marks said. He stood by the fireplace, the flickering flames and glowing coals behind him casting a reddish glow on the back of his black suit trousers. He seemed genial, relaxed, and I wondered how much of an act this was, designed to put us all at ease before springing his trap.

The drawing room seemed very full; no wonder, as there were so many people gathered there. Dorothy and Michael sat together on one of the sofas. Raymond sat opposite them in the brown leather armchair. Mrs. Weston, Ethel and I stood in a row over by the wall, our hands folded respectfully in front of us. Andrew stood to attention over by the door, with Doctor Goodfried beside him. Verity stood behind the sofa on which Dorothy and Michael sat. She kept catching my eye and managing to convey what she was thinking without uttering a word or even moving a muscle on her face. She was wearing black tonight. It felt appropriate.

Inspector Marks looked at each of us in turn, in silence, and then began speaking again. "There is one more person who'll be joining us. I'll wait until they arrive before I begin."

A ripple of interest flowed about the room. Who could he mean? Even as Dorothy bent to murmur in Michael's ear, I could hear the sound of a car engine outside and the crunch of tyres on the gravel driveway.

A few minutes later, there was a polite knock on the door. It opened when Inspector Marks bade whoever it was to come in. Constable Palmer came in first and following him was somebody nobody had expected to see – Arabella Ashford.

There was a cry of "Darling! You're back. Thank *God*," from Dorothy. Michael gave Arabella a strained, rather embarrassed smile. Raymond all but rolled his eyes. I felt Mrs Weston flinch a little next to me, but the moment passed too quickly before I could observe any of the rest of the people in the room.

Arabella looked pale and subdued. She wasn't handcuffed, but Constable Palmer had a hand on her arm. He supported her to an empty chair and she sat down and gazed at the floor in what looked like mute misery. She hadn't responded to Dorothy's words.

Inspector Marks waited for a moment before he spoke again. Before he did, he sought my gaze and we exchanged a moment of silent understanding. My stomach flipped.

"This has been an odd case," Inspector Marks said eventually, almost as if he were musing to himself. "Very odd, indeed. Nothing has been quite what it seemed." He rocked back and forward gently on his heels, smiling at each of us. "For one thing, when we keep referring to you all as a family, that's quite wrong, isn't it? Miss Ashford was not the natural daughter of Mrs Ashford. Miss Drew is only very distantly connected with the family. Mr Bentham is of no relation whatsoever, and Mr Harrison—" Inspector Marks coughed a little and took a sip from the water glass he had put on the mantelpiece. "I'm so sorry, excuse me. As I was saying, Mr Harrison is probably the only one here who could truly be said to belong to the Ashford family, as the nephew of the late Mrs Ashford."

I half expected Dorothy to say something sardonic at this point, something like *we know all this, Inspector, what is your point?* But she remained silent, her gaze on his tall, dark figure in front of the leaping flames. I realised then that Michael was holding her hand.

Inspector Marks went on. "Mrs Constance Bartleby, of course, was the sister in law of Mrs Ashford, the wife of her late brother. A relative but not related by birth."

That was all he said but the names of the two

dead women seemed to hang in the air for a moment before dissolving away. Arabella still stared dully at the carpet. For an uneasy moment, I wondered about her reason, her state of mind. Had her arrest and subsequent imprisonment in the police station broken her? Was that the reason she had confessed?

Listen to Inspector Marks, Joan. You don't know it all.

I took heed of my own stern warning and turned my attention back to the inspector. He was about to say something else when Raymond Bentham interrupted him with a loud and irritated sigh. "Look, is there a point to this – this *performance,* at all? This whole bally case has got absolutely nothing to do with me, and I'm sick to the back teeth of having to stay in this godforsaken spot whilst the police seem to be able to do nothing about catching the damned killer."

Inspector Marks seemed unperturbed by Raymond's outburst. He directed a small smile his way and continued speaking. "I appreciate your concern, Mr Bentham, and I won't take up a great deal of your time – of anyone's time, come to that. But it's important, I think, to clear this matter up once and for all, don't you agree? Then the innocent can have nothing more to fear – and no reason more to remain here – and the guilty can be suitably... punished."

The tension in the room leapt up another notch

as he finished his sentence. I watched Arabella's bovine expression twitch into something else, just for a moment. Dorothy and Michael exchanged uneasy glances. Raymond sat back in his chair, his black brows lowered over his eyes in a way that was most forbidding.

Inspector Marks let the tension sing for a moment longer. The snap and crackle of the flames behind him seemed very loud in the silent room. Then he began to speak again, quietly but with an air that commanded everyone's attention. "Almost everyone in this house had a reason to desire Mrs Ashford's death, or if not to actively desire it, to realise that they would benefit from her demise, whenever it came about."

Another beat of silence. I shifted a little, easing my feet which were aching in my shoes. The room was very warm, and I could feel my fingers slipping against one another as I held them clasped and still before me. I wondered when Inspector Marks would pull the rabbit from the hat. I knew, from watching him before, that there was a streak of theatricality in him that made him wait for the most dramatic moment possible.

He certainly had everyone's attention. I could hear Mrs Weston's breathing beside me, faster and more shallow than normal. I felt a spasm of pity for her. Poor Mrs Weston. Whatever happened now, things in Hidden House would never be the same again.

Inspector Marks was speaking again. "Now, the murder of Mrs Ashford was an unusual crime. Oh, yes—" He directed this last remark at Dorothy, whose head came up sharply at the word *murder*. "Yes, Miss Drew, murder it was. But a strange one. It was at once spontaneous and it was long planned. It was supposed to look like an accident. Both times it was supposed to look like an accident."

Both times? I knew what he meant but even I was getting confused. Raymond's expression moved from anger back to its more familiar boredom. Doctor Goodfried frowned. Arabella remained staring at the floor.

"Two attempts were made on the life of Mrs Ashford," Inspector Marks continued. He turned to face the dancing flames in the fireplace and then turned back. "*Two* attempts. When the first didn't succeed, a second attempt took place and this was successful. Mrs Ashford died."

I wondered if he were going to start to talk about motive, about the will and the confusion there, but he didn't. He fell silent once more, looking around the room at the different faces. Then he cleared his throat and went on. "Of course, what really threw the investigation was a fundamental error of judgement, and for that I blame myself entirely." He looked up and caught my eye. "Joan, would you like to say something?"

Even though we'd rehearsed this, I could still feel myself start and blush. There was a mutter from Michael and a frank stare from Raymond. A moment later, he said, "Why the hell would we want to hear her opinion on the subject? Might I remind you, Inspector, that she's a bally *cook*?"

"Miss Hart works with me," Inspector Marks said calmly, and there was another collective intake of breath around the room. I caught Verity's eye and she dropped me a lightning fast wink before her face settled into neutrality again. I was reminded of the time, a few years ago now, when I'd pretended to be an undercover police woman. And now here Inspector Marks was, pretending the same! If the room hadn't been so fraught with tension, I'd have laughed.

"Go on, Miss Hart," said the inspector.

I pulled myself together. "There were two murderers." That was why I had been reminded so strongly of the events at Merisham Lodge. And at Asharton Manor too, although as I admitted to myself, I'd got that bit wrong. Still, I wasn't a mind-reader.

"Miss Hart is right," said Inspector Marks. "There were two killers. Where I made my error of judgement was in assuming, quite naturally, that these two killers were working together."

Silence fell. A log shifted position in the fireplace, and the resulting soft noise was enough to make everyone start.

"These killers were *not* working together," said Inspector Marks. "Murderer one, if I may use the term, attempted to kill Mrs Ashford by giving her arsenic."

Arabella gave a sob. It was the first time she'd made a recognisable sound.

"So, it *was* you," Michael exclaimed. "I knew I'd seen you put something in Aunt Margaret's coffee. I *knew* it."

"Thank you, Mr Harrison," said the inspector, with steel in his tone. "Miss Ashford has already confessed to the crime." He looked at Arabella, white and weeping, and said in a gentler tone, "It was a moment of madness, perhaps. You knew your mother was about to disinherit you, or she had certainly threatened to. You also knew that, without money, you had no chance of retaining, or even perhaps gaining, the affection of Mr Bentham, who, I think it fair to say, you are very much in love with."

Arabella's white cheeks stained pink. She hung her head. Raymond stared at her with something like horror, possibly the most authentic expression his face had ever worn.

"You saw that Mr Harrison had brought wild mushrooms with him that afternoon, for the dinner table, as he often did. You've told me that you believed everyone would think any illness resulting that evening would be from *mushroom* poisoning, not from the poisoning of the coffee pot that evening. You made sure to drink some yourself, to add credence to the idea that you were an innocent victim of the so-called food poisoning that you were sure would have killed or severely incapacitated Mrs Ashford."

"I didn't mean to kill her," Arabella cried. She shook her hair free from her tear-stained face. "I promise you it's the truth. I never meant for her to die."

"Mrs Ashford was very elderly and she was an invalid," Inspector Marks said sternly. "You knew that such an action would have very likely resulted in her death. Not to mention the fact that you put the lives of several innocent people at risk."

He stopped talking for a moment and the only sound in the room was that of Arabella's sobs and the crackle of the dying fire. It needed more wood, but now was not the time for me to concern myself with that. I could feel the knot of anxiety tying itself tighter in my stomach.

Dorothy spoke up then. I scarcely recognised her voice, it was so tremulous and quiet. "So, if it wasn't Arabella, who is the second murderer?"

"I'm coming to that, Miss Drew." Inspector Marks began to pace again, slowly. "The night of

Mrs Ashford's death – forgive me, the night *before* Mrs Ashford's death – she had an argument with Miss Ashford. The upshot of the argument was that Mrs Ashford was determined to change her will in favour of her sister-in-law and companion, Mrs Bartleby. The argument was overheard by Mrs Bartleby herself, and she immediately, or as soon as she could, informed the other person involved in this crime. Murderer Number Two."

"So, it wasn't Mrs Bartleby," Dorothy exclaimed. We all looked at her in surprise, but she seemed too astonished to be embarrassed. "But, I thought—"

"Mrs Bartleby knew nothing about the murder," said Inspector Marks. He sounded sad for a moment. "She was foolish in the extreme to let slip to her...companion, let us say, what she knew. But I don't believe she did so because she realised what they would do in the light of that knowledge. I think she was just, naturally, delighted at the idea of inheriting a great deal of money and wanted to share her good fortune with...shall we say, someone who meant a great deal to her."

Inspector Marks reached the edge of the Persian rug and pivoted slowly to turn back the way he'd walked. "Murderer Number Two, who was a great deal more intelligent, quick thinking and ruthless than either Miss Ashford or poor Mrs Bartleby, realised that this was a chance. A chance to get hold of a great deal of money and in such a way that was almost without suspicion. It very nearly did work, and it would have, if it hadn't been for Miss Hart's sharp eyes noticing that Mrs Ashford's body had been moved." He looked up and caught my eye. He inclined his head.

I took up the thread of the tale. I wished Verity was standing next to me, side by side, rather than across the room. "Mrs Ashford's death was at first attributed to mushroom or food poisoning. Then, when we realised that none of the mushrooms used in the soup that night were poisonous at all, the police began to look more closely at her cause of death."

"Why, of course they weren't poisonous," Michael cried indignantly. "As if I'd be stupid enough to pick the wrong kind—"

"Thank you, Mr Harrison," Inspector Marks said, cutting him off. "We're quite aware that you had no intention of making everyone ill that night. You simply wanted to bring some fresh produce to your aunt, like you often did. You have nothing to blame yourself for, that night."

"Well, quite," Michael muttered, looking offended. Dorothy gave him a dig in the ribs and he piped down.

Inspector Marks gave him a long, silent glance. I could feel my heart thudding against my rib cage. "I said, you had nothing to blame yourself for, *that* night, Mr Harrison."

Michael looked confused. "What do you mean?"

Inspector Marks leant forward, his eyes fixed upon Michael's face. "I mean, Mr Harrison, in the matter of arsenic poisoning, you are entirely innocent."

"Well, yes, of course—"

Inspector Marks pressed on relentlessly. "Whereas you are entirely guilty of causing the death of Mrs Ashford by a blow to the head, skilfully and quickly done, of rearranging the body to conceal the wound, and later on, of causing the death of Constance Bartleby by cyanide poisoning."

Chapter Twenty-Nine

THE SILENCE THAT FOLLOWED THIS last sentence of the inspector's lasted a full thirty seconds. It may have been longer. I was preoccupied in watching Michael's face.

Eventually, he gave a dreadful laugh. "*What*?"

Inspector Marks straightened up. "You killed your elderly aunt and then you killed her sister-in-law, Mrs Constance Bartleby."

Beside Michael, Dorothy had gone white to the lips. The lipstick on her mouth had been licked or bitten away. "What? Inspector...this can't be right—"

Inspector Marks looked honestly apologetic. "I'm sorry, Miss Drew."

"This is *ludicrous*," Michael said, beginning to sound angry. "Absolutely ludicrous. You must be mad." He lurched forward as if he were about to get up out of his seat. "I'm not sitting here for a moment longer, listening to these *absurd* allegations."

Constable Palmer, who up until now had been

waiting unobtrusively in a corner of the room, stepped forward. Michael stopped moving.

"Just sit back down, Mr Harrison," Inspector Marks said.

Michael reluctantly did so. He had a strained smile on his face, as if reaching for a queasy sort of casualness, but his eyes were flickering from side to side as if planning an escape. I tensed a little more, but Inspector Marks had seen it too. He stepped in front of him.

"This is just ridiculous," said Michael. He was sweating. "Why on earth would I want to kill my aunt? And Constance?"

"Oh, that's easy," said the inspector. "You were due to inherit a great deal of money."

"No, I wasn't—"

Inspector Marks leant forward. "What are you studying at Cambridge, Mr Harrison?"

Michael said nothing. I saw the tip of his tongue flicker out to moisten his top lip.

"Mr Harrison?"

Michael remained silent. Inspector Marks sighed and straightened up, looking over at Raymond Bentham.

"Mr Bentham, what is Mr Harrison studying at Cambridge?"

Raymond looked as though he'd been hit in the face with something heavy. At another prompt from the inspector, he shook his head slightly and said, hoarsely, "Chemistry."

"Precisely." Inspector Marks turned his attention back to Michael. "You're a chemistry student, Michael. You knew very well what your erstwhile cousin had put in your aunt's coffee, didn't you? If you hadn't worked it out when you observed her doing it, you knew damn well that everyone was suffering from arsenic poisoning, including yourself. Coupled with the fact that Constance Bartleby was about to inherit the majority of Mrs Ashford's fortune – or so you both thought – it was the perfect opportunity. You knew, if anyone, that Arabella would come under suspicion. In fact, perhaps that was an added incentive? If it's discovered that Mrs Ashford did die a suspicious death, and her adopted daughter is arrested and then charged, why, the other beneficiary of the original will gains even more when Miss Ashford is hanged for murder."

Arabella shuddered, squeezing her eyes shut. I'd scarcely noticed Dorothy for the past few minutes but when I looked at her now, she looked as though she were about to be overtaken by nausea. I think Verity noticed too, because she stepped forward a little anxiously.

Michael tried one last time. "All of this is very amusing," he said, with a sneer that trembled. "But it still means nothing to me. I don't know what you mean by me inheriting a lot of money. It's ludicrous. Aunt Margaret only left me a mere five thousand."

247

He turned the sneer in my direction. "No doubt that's an incredible fortune to someone like *you*."

Despite my having these exact thoughts, I still flinched a little. I could see Verity standing behind him looking as though she was about to clobber him. I shook my head at her very slightly.

Inspector Marks didn't defend me. Instead he turned to me and raised his eyebrows.

We'd practiced this moment too. I could feel the rustle of paper in my apron pocket and put my hand in to draw it out, along with the other, much smaller object.

"Constance Bartleby was set to inherit a large fortune," I said, stepping forward.

"And?" Michael practically spat the word at me.

I opened up the folded piece of paper in front of him, so he could read it. "And you were married to her, Mr Harrison. To Constance Bartleby. You got married last year."

Beside him, Dorothy jerked forward, her hand going to her mouth, almost retching. Michael didn't react, gazing in horror at the marriage certificate in my hands.

"I told her to—" he half whispered.

Inspector Marks pounced. "Told her to do what, Mr Harrison? Burn it? Women don't burn marriage certificates, any more than they burn love letters." At this, Michael looked up, his face contorting with rage. So, he'd written her letters too? Inspector

Marks and I exchanged a glance. Michael wasn't to know that we hadn't found them yet.

"Of all the goddam—" A perfect string of unrepeatable curse words followed. Michael leant forward to rip the certificate from my hands, but I'd been expecting him to do that and jumped nimbly back out of the way.

"Be quiet." Inspector Marks nodded to Constable Palmer, who approached with a set of handcuffs. "Naturally, given that Constance could have spilled the beans about your...unorthodox relationship at any moment, and the fact that her death meant that as her legal husband, you would inherit her estate, she had to be silenced too. That was a little sloppy, Mr Harrison. Not very convincing after all. I suppose it was the best you could do at the time."

Silence fell. Michael's face was so dark with rage, his golden good looks buried under a mask of anger. I could scarcely look at him.

Then Dorothy spoke. She sounded broken, her voice trembling, her body shivering. "No – no, I can't – this doesn't make sense, Inspector."

Inspector Marks looked at her with compassion. "I'm very sorry, Miss Drew."

"No, it's just—" She stopped herself, swallowed painfully. "It's just... I don't understand. The night that – the night Constance died—" She stopped speaking, a slow tide of colour rising up in her face. She looked up at Inspector Marks as if pleading for her life. "He – Michael – was with me that night. The whole night." She looked over at Michael, her face aghast. "You were, weren't you?"

Michael went to say something, but we never found out what. Inspector Marks spoke over him, and his tone was extra gentle. "I'm sorry, Miss Drew. But Michael left you that evening, in plenty of time to go to Constance Bartleby's room. He had ample time to kill her."

"No," said Dorothy brokenly. "No, I—"

"I'm sorry, Miss Drew. But *I* know that you can't remember." Inspector Marks paused. "You were... indisposed."

Everyone in the room knew what he really meant. Dorothy hung her head so that the smooth golden curtains of hair on either side of her face fell to cover her flaming cheeks. I saw tears begin to fall into her lap.

Inspector Marks stood back and nodded to Constable Palmer. I stepped back to stand with Mrs Weston and Ethel, my heart beginning to return to a normal rhythm. We all listened in silence as Inspector Marks began to speak the words of the caution to Michael Harrison and to Arabella Ashford. When he'd finished speaking, there was nothing but silence in the room, punctuated by Dorothy's sobs and the crackle and spit of the last flaming log in the fire.

Chapter Thirty

WHEN CONSTABLE PALMER AND INSPECTOR Marks took Michael and Arabella away, the rest of us remained in the drawing room for a moment longer. We were as still and as silent as statues, all stunned by recent events, even those of us who had known what to expect. Verity was the first to move. She bent down to Dorothy, who sat white and aghast, as if turned to stone in her seat. I couldn't hear what Verity said to her but, after a moment, she held out her hands and helped Dorothy to her feet. Our mistress staggered, and Verity braced herself against her more firmly. Doctor Goodfried hurried to assist her and they both supported Dorothy in leaving the room. I could hear her fumbling footsteps and theirs making their way up the stairs in the hallway outside. I took a moment to send a fervent prayer up to the heavens that the doctor would be able to give her a sedative of some sort. Otherwise, I had a feeling Verity and I would need to hide all the brandy bottles in the house tonight.

Mrs Weston walked unsteadily to the door and paused with her hand on the door handle. Then she turned to catch my eye. Her own were brimming with tears. "Joan—"

"Yes, Mrs Weston?" I tried to sound as gentle and as supportive as I could.

Mrs Weston closed her eyes for a brief moment. She looked bludgeoned by the events of the last hour, dark hollows beneath her eyes, a muscle spasming in her cheek. "I'm – I'm going to my room. Please... Please take over. I'm leaving the house in your hands for the evening."

I nodded. I knew a part of me was supposed to be pleased that she thought highly enough of me to give me the responsibility, but most of me just felt impatient. I didn't want to cook anymore. I wanted to work with Inspector Marks. *Not just* work *with him, Joan*, said that sly little demon of a voice inside me and I mentally batted it away.

After the door shut behind the housekeeper, I looked over at Ethel and resisted the urge to shut her jaw with a finger. Instead I nudged her.

There was the rustle from the leather armchair. I'd almost forgotten Raymond was in the room. He was rubbing his jaw as if checking for stubble or as if he had toothache. He caught my eye and opened his mouth.

"Joan. Could you get me...""

I didn't say anything. I just held his gaze until

his voice petered out and he cleared his throat. He looked – could it be? – wary of me. For the first time in my life, I felt a tingle of power.

Raymond switched his gaze to Ethel. "Ethel, could you get me a brandy. A large one?" I saw him glance back at me and then he added, hastily, "Please?"

I left them to it and went downstairs to the kitchen.

WHEN I GOT THERE, I stood for a moment looking about me. At the scrubbed kitchen table, where we'd eaten so many meals. The dresser stacked with china. The copper pots hanging above the range. The larder and the pantry. The huge, pot-bellied flour barrel. The little jelly moulds twinkled like jewels in the electric light.

I supposed there was much to do – when wasn't there? But at that moment, I didn't feel like doing anything. The whole room suddenly had a sort of artifice, as if it were a stage set or a display in a department store. It didn't seem real.

I sat down at the table, feeling flat. More than flat – adrift. As if I didn't know my purpose any more. What was I going to do?

There was the sound of quick footsteps on the stairs outside and then Verity came into the kitchen. She looked serious but not unduly worried.

"V!" I got up and threw my arms around her. Unsurprised, she hugged me back. "How is Dorothy?"

"Out cold in her bed."

"Not already?"

Incredibly, Verity giggled. "Oh, no, not like *that*, Joan. Thank goodness. The doctor gave her something to help her sleep. She's had an awful shock."

"Poor Dorothy." I honestly pitied her from the bottom of my heart. "But then, V, think what a lucky escape she's had. Imagine if she'd gone ahead and married Michael. Think of what might have happened."

"I know." Verity collapsed onto one of the kitchen chairs with a groan. "For a start, she'd have been bigamously married."

"That would hardly have been the biggest problem," I said, thinking of what Michael had done to his wife.

"I know *that*. I don't think that's occurred to Dorothy just yet. Well, it can't have done. She's still reeling."

"I'm glad she's getting some rest."

"Me too." Verity pushed her hands through the red curls of her hair and yawned. "Anyway, I had a word with Doctor Goodfried. He recommended a very good place near London that can cure – well, you know – *help* people who have this problem. Dorothy's problem."

"What kind of place?" I asked, curiously.

"Sanatorium. It's very effective, apparently. Costs the earth, but it's not as though Dorothy can't afford it."

"Do you think she would go?"

Verity pondered, pushing her bottom lip out. "Do you know, I think she might."

"Well, let's hope so."

Verity yawned again. "Golly, I'm tired. I think I might turn in, now that Dorothy won't need me." She pushed herself upright. "And you, Joanie? What's to become of you?"

"What do you mean?"

Verity smiled in a tired fashion. "Well, now that you *work for* Inspector Marks..."

I could feel my face heating up. "He was only saying that to get them to listen to me."

"Hmm. Possibly." Verity braced herself and stood up. "Well, my dear old friend, I'm off to bed. Adventures new, tomorrow or soon, for both of us, perhaps. And your play! Who knows what might happen?"

For a moment, we stood facing each other across the table. I could feel that old cord of affection and understanding binding us together and knew that it would always be there, in some way, no matter what happened, no matter in what different directions our life path led.

"Good night, Miss Hart," Verity said, grinning.

"Good night, Miss Hunter," I retorted, smiling back. She winked at me and was gone.

I LISTENED TO HER FOOTSTEPS climbing the stairs and then walking above me in the hallway. I sighed, stretched, and untied my apron, hanging it by the pantry. To hell with the breakfasts; to hell with the work remaining this evening. I, Joan Hart, was going to bed.

I was walking towards the back door, intending to lock it up for the night when it suddenly opened inwards, making me start.

"Oh! Inspector Marks." I told myself to calm myself. He was clearly just here to – what was the word? – *debrief* me on our successful conclusion to the case.

"Hello, Joan." He took his hat from his head and smiled at me.

I took my courage in my hands. "Hello, Tom."

"I'm probably interrupting you—"

"No, please, come in. I was just—" I stopped myself and gestured instead toward a chair.

"I can't stop for longer than a minute, I'm afraid." Inspector Marks looked sincerely regretful. I felt my heart begin a slow but pleasurable thudding. "I know we have a lot to talk about, and I can't thank you enough for your assistance just now—"

"It was nothing. I just followed your lead."

"Well, I have to go to the station now. It's going to be a long night. But I just wanted..." He looked down at the hands clasping his hat for a moment. Then he looked up, straight into my eyes. "I just wanted to know if – if you'd like to have dinner with me. Tomorrow night. If that's possible. If you want to."

A foolish smile wanted to spread itself across my face, and I had to fight down a nervous, schoolgirlish giggle. I took a deep breath, wanting to remain calm. I was quite proud of myself. "Yes, thank you, Tom. I'd love to."

"Good. Let's talk tomorrow then." Inspector Marks put his hat firmly back on his head. He looked as if he wanted to shake my hand – or do something similar – but he caught my eye again and we both smiled a smile at each other that was both encompassing and a little sheepish.

"'Until tomorrow then," I said, still calm although my heart was singing inside me.

"Good night, Joan."

"Good night." I watched him walk over to the back door and waited. He turned at the door to give me one last smile, one that warmed me to the tips of my toes. Then he nodded and left, shutting the kitchen door behind him.

THE END

ENJOYED THIS BOOK? AN HONEST review left at Amazon and Goodreads is always welcome and really important for indie authors. The more reviews an independently published book has, the easier it is to market it and find new readers.

Want some more of Celina Grace's work for free? Subscribers to her mailing list get a free digital copy of **Requiem (A Kate Redman Mystery: Book 2)**, a free digital copy of A Prescription for Death **(The Asharton Manor Mysteries Book 2)** and a free PDF copy of her short story collection **A Blessing From The Obeah Man.**

Requiem (A Kate Redman Mystery: Book 2)

WHEN THE BODY OF TROUBLED teenager Elodie Duncan is pulled from the river in Abbeyford, the case is at first assumed to be a straightforward suicide. Detective Sergeant Kate Redman is shocked to discover that she'd met the victim the night before her death, introduced by Kate's younger brother Jay. As the case develops, it becomes clear that Elodie was murdered. A talented young musician, Elodie had been keeping some strange company and was hiding her own dark secrets.

As the list of suspects begin to grow, so do the questions. What is the significance of the painting Elodie modelled for? Who is the man who was seen with her on the night of her death? Is there any connection with another student's death at the exclusive musical college that Elodie attended?

As Kate and her partner Detective Sergeant Mark Olbeck attempt to unravel the mystery, the dark undercurrents of the case threaten those whom Kate holds most dear...

A Prescription for Death (The Asharton Manor Mysteries: Book 2) – a novella

"I HAD A SURGE OF kinship the first time I saw the manor, perhaps because we'd both seen better days."

It is 1947. Asharton Manor, once one of the most beautiful stately homes in the West Country, is now a convalescent home for former soldiers. Escaping the devastation of post-war London is Vivian Holt, who moves to the nearby village and begins to volunteer as a nurse's aide at the manor. Mourning the death of her soldier husband, Vivian finds solace in her new friendship with one of the older patients, Norman Winter, someone who has served his country in both world wars. Slowly, Vivian's heart begins to heal, only to be torn apart when she arrives for work one day to be told that Norman is dead.

It seems a straightforward death, but is it? Why did a particular photograph disappear from Norman's possessions after his death? Who is the sinister figure who keeps following Vivian? Suspicion and doubts begin to grow and when another death occurs, Vivian begins to realise that the war may be over but the real battle is just beginning...

A Blessing From The Obeah Man

DARE YOU READ ON? HORRIFYING, scary, sad and thought-provoking, this short story collection will take you on a macabre journey. In the titular story, a honeymooning couple take a wrong turn on their trip around Barbados. The Mourning After brings you a shivery story from a suicidal teenager. In Freedom Fighter, an unhappy middle-aged man chooses the wrong day to make a bid for freedom, whereas Little Drops of Happiness and Wave Goodbye are tales of darkness from sunny Down Under. Strapping Lass and The Club are for those who prefer, shall we say, a little meat to the story...

JUST GO TO CELINA'S WEBSITE to sign up. It's quick, easy and free. Be the first to be informed of promotions, giveaways, new releases and subscriber-only benefits by subscribing to her (occasional) newsletter.

Aspiring or new authors might like to check out Celina's other site http://www.indieauthorschool. com for motivation, inspiration and advice on writing and publishing a book, or even starting a whole new career as an indie author. Get a free eBook, a mini e-course, cheat sheets and other helpful downloads when you sign up for the newsletter.

http://www.celinagrace.com
http://www.indieauthorschool.com
Twitter: @celina__grace
Facebook: http://www.facebook.
com/authorcelinagrace

HAVE YOU READ THE FIRST Asharton Manor Mystery? This is the book that introduces Joan and Verity and it's available for a mere 99 cents:

Death at the Manor (The Asharton Manor Mysteries: Book 1)

Please note – this is a novella-length piece of fiction – not a full length novel

IT IS 1929. ASHARTON MANOR stands alone in the middle of a pine forest, once the place where ancient pagan ceremonies were undertaken in honour of the goddess Astarte. The Manor is one of the most beautiful stately homes in the West Country and seems like a palace to Joan Hart, newly arrived from London to take up a servant's position as the head kitchen maid. Getting to grips with her new role and with her fellow workers, Joan is kept busy, but not too busy to notice that the glittering surface of life at the Manor might be hiding some dark secrets. The beautiful and wealthy mistress of the house, Delphine Denford, keeps falling ill but why? Confiding her thoughts to her friend and fellow housemaid, feisty Verity Hunter, Joan is unsure of what exactly is making her uneasy, but then Delphine Denford dies...

Armed only with their own good sense and quick thinking, Joan and Verity must pit their wits against a cunning murderer in order to bring them to justice.

Download Death at the Manor from
Amazon Kindle, available now.

Other books in the Miss Hart and
Miss Hunter Investigate series:

MURDER AT MERISHAM LODGE (BOOK 1)

A mansion, a title and marriage to a wealthy Lord – Lady Eveline Cartwright has it all. Unfortunately, it's not enough to prevent her being bludgeoned to death one night in the study of Merisham Lodge, the family's country estate in Derbyshire.

Suspicion quickly falls on her ne'er-do-well son, Peter, but not everyone in the household is convinced of his guilt. Head kitchen maid Joan Hart and lady's maid, Verity Hunter, know that when it comes to a crime, all is not always as it seems.

With suspicions and motives thick on the ground, Joan and Verity must use all the wit and courage they possess to expose a deadly murderer who will stop at nothing to achieve their aim...

Available now from Amazon exclusively.

DEATH AT THE THEATRE (BOOK 2)

London, 1932. Kitchen maid, Joan Hart, and lady's maid, Verity Hunter, intend to enjoy their trip to the theatre, especially as Verity's uncle Tommy is one of the leading men in the play. Unfortunately, Act Two of the play is curtailed when the lights come up in the interval, and the girls realise a man has been stabbed to death almost under their very noses.

The case reunites the servant sleuths with their old ally, Detective Inspector Marks, and whilst the girls do their best to solve the case whilst keeping their jobs, the glitter and glamour of the theatre may prove to be as dangerous as any battlefield...

Available now from Amazon exclusively.

Other books by Celina Grace

Interested in historical mysteries?

The Asharton Manor Mysteries

SOME OLD HOUSES HAVE MORE history than others...

The Asharton Manor Mysteries Boxed Set is a four part series of novellas spanning the twentieth century. Each standalone story (about 20,000 words) uses Asharton Manor as the backdrop to a devious and twisting crime mystery. The boxed set includes the following stories:

Death at the Manor

IT IS 1929. ASHARTON MANOR stands alone in the middle of a pine forest, once the place where ancient pagan ceremonies were undertaken in honour of the goddess Astarte. The Manor is one of the most beautiful stately homes in the West Country and seems like a palace to Joan Hart, newly arrived from London to take up a servant's position as the head kitchen maid. Getting to grips with her new role and with her fellow workers, Joan is kept busy, but not too busy to notice that the glittering surface of life at the Manor might be hiding some dark secrets. The beautiful and wealthy mistress of the house, Delphine Denford, keeps falling ill but why? Confiding her thoughts to her friend and fellow housemaid Verity Hunter, Joan is unsure of what exactly is making her uneasy, but then Delphine Denford dies... Armed only with their own good sense and quick thinking, Joan and Verity must pit their wits against a cunning murderer in order to bring them to justice.

A Prescription for Death

IT IS 1947. ASHARTON MANOR, once one of the most beautiful stately homes in the West Country, is now a convalescent home for former soldiers. Escaping the devastation of post-war London is Vivian Holt, who moves to the nearby village and begins to volunteer as a nurse's aide at the manor. Mourning the death of her soldier husband, Vivian finds solace in her new friendship with one of the older patients, Norman Winter, someone who has served his country in both world wars. Slowly, Vivian's heart begins to heal, only to be torn apart when she arrives for work one day to be told that Norman is dead. It seems a straightforward death, but is it? Why did a particular photograph disappear from Norman's possessions after his death? Who is the sinister figure who keeps following Vivian? Suspicion and doubts begin to grow and when another death occurs, Vivian begins to realise that the war may be over but the real battle is just beginning...

The Rhythm of Murder

IT IS 1973. EVE AND Janey, two young university students, are en route to a Bristol commune when they take an unexpected detour to the little village of Midford. Seduced by the roguish charms of a young man who picks them up in the village pub, they are astonished to find themselves at Asharton Manor, now the residence of the very wealthy, very famous, very degenerate Blue Turner, lead singer of rock band Dirty Rumours. The golden summer rolls on, full of sex, drugs and rock and roll, but Eve begins to sense that there may be a sinister side to all the hedonism. And then one day, Janey disappears, seemingly run away... but as Eve begins to question what happened to her friend, she realises that she herself might be in terrible danger...

Number Thirteen, Manor Close

IT IS 2014. BEATRICE AND Mike Dunhill are finally moving into a house of their own, Number Thirteen, Manor Close. Part of the brand new Asharton Estate, Number Thirteen is built on the remains of the original Asharton Manor which was destroyed in a fire in 1973. Still struggling a little from the recent death of her mother, Beatrice is happy to finally have a home of her own – until she begins to experience some strange happenings that, try as she might, she can't explain away. Her husband Mike seems unconvinced and only her next door neighbour Mia seems to understand Beatrice's growing fear of her home. Uncertain of her own judgement, Beatrice must confront what lies beneath the beautiful surface of the Asharton Estate. But can she do so without losing her mind – or her life?

Available now exclusively from Amazon.

Have you met Detective
Sergeant Kate Redman?

THE KATE REDMAN MYSTERIES ARE the bestselling
detective mysteries from Celina Grace, featuring the
flawed but determined female officer Kate Redman
and her pursuit of justice in the West Country town
of Abbeyford.

Hushabye (A Kate Redman Mystery: Book 1) is
the novel that introduces Detective Sergeant Kate
Redman on her first case in Abbeyford. It's available
for **free**!

A missing baby. A murdered girl. A case where
everyone has something to hide...

On the first day of her new job in the West
Country, Detective Sergeant Kate Redman finds
herself investigating the kidnapping of Charlie
Fullman, the newborn son of a wealthy entrepreneur
and his trophy wife. It seems a straightforward
case... but as Kate and her fellow officer Mark
Olbeck delve deeper, they uncover murky secrets
and multiple motives for the crime.

Kate finds the case bringing up painful memories of
her own past secrets. As she confronts the truth about
herself, her increasing emotional instability threatens
both her hard-won career success and the possibility
that they will ever find Charlie Fullman alive...

Hushabye (A Kate Redman Mystery: Book 1)

ON THE FIRST DAY OF her new job in the West Country, Detective Sergeant Kate Redman finds herself investigating the kidnapping of Charlie Fullman, the newborn son of a wealthy entrepreneur and his trophy wife. It seems a straightforward case... but as Kate and her fellow officer Mark Olbeck delve deeper, they uncover murky secrets and multiple motives for the crime.

Kate finds the case bringing up painful memories of her own past secrets. As she confronts the truth about herself, her increasing emotional instability threatens both her hard-won career success and the possibility that they will ever find Charlie Fullman alive...

Hushabye is the book that introduces
Detective Sergeant Kate Redman.
Available as a FREE download
from Amazon Kindle.

CELINA GRACE'S PSYCHOLOGICAL THRILLER, LOST **Girls** is also available from Amazon:

Twenty-three years ago, Maudie Sampson's childhood friend Jessica disappeared on a family holiday in Cornwall. She was never seen again.

In the present day, Maudie is struggling to come to terms with the death of her wealthy father, her increasingly fragile mental health and a marriage that's under strain. Slowly, she becomes aware that there is someone following her: a blonde woman in a long black coat with an intense gaze. As the woman begins to infiltrate her life, Maudie realises no one else appears to be able to see her.

Is Maudie losing her mind? Is the woman a figment of her imagination or does she actually exist? Have the sins of the past caught up with Maudie's present...or is there something even more sinister going on?

Lost Girls is a novel from the author of The House on Fever Street: a dark and convoluted tale which proves that nothing can be taken for granted and no-one is as they seem.

Currently available on Amazon.

THE HOUSE ON FEVER STREET is the first psychological thriller by Celina Grace.

Thrown together in the aftermath of the London bombings of 2005, Jake and Bella embark on a passionate and intense romance. Soon Bella is living with Jake in his house on Fever Street, along with his sardonic brother Carl and Carl's girlfriend, the beautiful but chilly Veronica.

As Bella tries to come to terms with her traumatic experience, her relationship with Jake also becomes a source of unease. Why do the housemates never go into the garden? Why does Jake have such bad dreams and such explosive outbursts of temper?

Bella is determined to understand the man she loves but as she uncovers long-buried secrets, is she putting herself back into mortal danger?

The House on Fever Street is the first psychological thriller from writer Celina Grace – a chilling study of the violent impulses that lurk beneath the surfaces of everyday life.

Shortlisted for the 2006 Crime Writers' Association Debut Dagger Award.

Currently available on Amazon.

Extra Special Thanks Are Due To My Wonderful Advance Readers Team…

THESE ARE MY 'SUPER READERS' who are kind enough to beta read my books, point out my more ridiculous mistakes, spot any typos that have slipped past my editor and best of all, write honest reviews in exchange for advance copies of my work. Many, many thanks to you all.

Acknowledgements

MANY THANKS TO ALL THE following splendid souls:

Chris Howard for the brilliant cover designs; Andrea Harding for editing and proofreading; Lifelong Schlockers and friends David Hall, Ben Robinson and Alberto Lopez; Ross McConnell for advice on police procedural and for also being a great brother; Kathleen and Pat McConnell, Anthony Alcock, Naomi White, Mo Argyle, Lee Benjamin, Bonnie Wede, Sherry and Amali Stoute, Cheryl and Mark Beckles, Georgia Lucas-Going, Steven Lucas, Loletha Stoute and Harry Lucas, Helen Parfect, Helen Watson, Emily Way, Sandy Hall, Kristýna Vosecká and of course my lovely Chris, Mabel, Jethro and Isaiah.

CPSIA information can be obtained
at www.ICGtesting.com
Printed in the USA
FSHW010744021218
54176FS